"What brought you to Montana?"

Thomas shrugged a bit defensively. "Opportunity. What else? I'd heard about this settlement and Montana was a place I'd never been to. The Yoders were looking for a bookkeeper. The rest is history."

The truth but not the whole truth, Emma thought. She instinctively knew he was leaving out huge chunks of what motivated him to leave his home behind and move fifteen hundred miles away.

But it was too early into their acquaintance to press. "What do you think of Montana so far?"

His eyes locked with hers. "It's everything I could hope for."

Oh yes, he was interested in courting. Emma could not deny it any more than she could deny Hannah's uncanny fondness for this man. But how did she feel about him? There was something of a mystery about Thomas. She wasn't about to let herself get overly fond of him—or worse, let her daughter become overly fond of him—without a thorough understanding of his character and motivation. And that included the elusive past he kept avoiding.

Living on a remote self-sufficient homestead in North Idaho, **Patrice Lewis** is a Christian wife, mother, author, blogger, columnist and speaker. She has practiced and written about rural subjects for almost thirty years. When she isn't writing, Patrice enjoys self-sufficiency projects, such as animal husbandry, small-scale dairy production, gardening, food preservation and canning, and homeschooling. She and her husband have been married since 1990 and have two daughters.

Books by Patrice Lewis

Love Inspired

The Amish Newcomer
Amish Baby Lessons
Her Path to Redemption
The Amish Animal Doctor
The Mysterious Amish Nanny
Their Road to Redemption

Visit the Author Profile page at LoveInspired.com.

Their Road to Redemption

Patrice Lewis

LOVE INSPIRED

INSPIRATIONAL ROMANCE

LOVE INSPIRED®
INSPIRATIONAL ROMANCE

ISBN-13: 978-1-335-58578-3

Their Road to Redemption

Copyright © 2023 by Patrice Lewis

For questions and comments about the quality of this book, please contact us at CustomerService@Harlequin.com.

Love Inspired
22 Adelaide St. West, 41st Floor
Toronto, Ontario M5H 4E3, Canada
www.LoveInspired.com

Printed in U.S.A.

Wherefore by their fruits ye shall know them.
—*Matthew* 7:20

To God, for blessing me
with my husband and daughters,
the best family anyone could hope for.

Chapter One

Thomas Kemp gazed out the window of the bus, gauging the region that would become his new home. The August heat shimmered on the rugged mountains of Montana's Bitterroot Range dominating the western horizon, while the wide valley at the base alternated between dense conifers and broad meadows. A narrow two-lane highway bisected the view and dry yellow grasses lined the roadway.

Unlike Indiana, which he'd left four days before, the population here was much thinner and more spread out. His destination was the town of Pierce, and it seemed a long way from anything else. A small part of him was thrilled at the upcoming adventure of settling in a new place. A bigger part wondered if he would be accepted by the startup Amish settlement toward which he was headed. It wasn't common for a church to bring a former jailbird like him into the fold.

Thomas fingered the scar on his left cheek, slashed open by the leader of the gang he'd been hanging with and the only visual remnant of his life of petty crime. He thanked *Gott* for the bishop's willingness to overlook his past, and for his Amish upbringing that now offered him the refuge he so desperately sought.

The compartments on the underside of the bus carried all his baggage: four heavy suitcases stuffed with all his worldly possessions. His journey here to Montana would allow him to begin anew, far away from the sins he had spent years committing.

Over the bus intercom came an announcement that Pierce was just ahead. Craning his neck to peer through the front windshield, Thomas saw scattered buildings that coalesced into a town still partially shielded by the cloak of conifers. He knew Pierce was small, no more than 3,500 people. Based on how remote it was, he suspected it was fairly self-contained. He smiled to himself. It seemed an excellent place for the Amish settlement that was, he now knew, attracting church members of an adventurous nature from all over the east and the Midwest where farmland was getting scarcer and more expensive.

At last, the bus pulled off the narrow two-lane highway into a tiny depot that was little more than a concrete apron with an awning and a few benches. Some people lingered near cars in the parking lot, obviously waiting for friends or loved ones. The main part of town lay just across the highway. With a pneumatic sigh, the doors opened and passengers began disembarking.

Thomas felt a moment's concern. The church's bishop had promised to meet him, but there was no Amish buggy in sight.

For fifteen minutes, the platform was busy as people claimed their luggage and reunited with those waiting for them. By the time the bus departed and the other passengers had left either by foot or by car, Thomas was left alone under the awning.

The edge of town lay intriguingly close. He could easily cross the rural two-lane highway and walk down the main street that lay perpendicular, but he was hindered by his suitcases. He didn't dare leave them behind and there was no place to store them.

Doubts flew down and settled on his shoulders. Was it all a massive joke? Maybe he didn't have a job waiting for him after all. Maybe the bishop had changed his mind about having such a shady character settle among them. Maybe there wasn't even an Amish settlement outside of town. He saw no evidence of any church members around. No familiar *kapps* or colorful dresses of the women, no straw hats and suspenders of men. Was he in the wrong place?

Thomas stood straight, closed his eyes and said a prayer. It was vague and had much to do with peace of mind and a sincere hope he hadn't been forgotten. Then he opened his eyes and strained his gaze down the street. Nothing.

Without any option, he set himself to wait. The metal bench was not the most comfortable, but its rigidity reminded him of the hard life he'd left behind.

He almost dozed.

Gradually, the familiar clip-clop sound of horse hooves penetrated his travel-weary brain. Thomas snapped upright and peered down the main street of the town. Yes, it was an Amish buggy pulled by a horse with a shining brown coat. But it wasn't an older man holding the reins, it was a young woman. He shook his head. It couldn't be his ride.

The woman pulled the horse to a stop on the other side of the deserted highway, looked both ways, then directed the buggy straight across the lanes and into the parking lot of the bus depot.

"Thomas Kemp?" she inquired. "Are you Thomas Kemp?"

Relief flooded his system. "*Ja,* I am."

"I'm Emma Fisher. I'm Bishop Beiler's niece. He was detained and couldn't come pick you up, so he asked if I could. I'm so sorry to be late."

He tried not to stare. He hadn't met many Amish women who could model in the *Englisch* world, but Emma could. Her dark, almost-black hair was tucked under her white *kapp*, which indicated her married status. She had chocolate-brown eyes and a beautiful smile. But beneath the stunning exterior, he detected a thread of steel. This, his instinct told him, was a woman not to be trifled with.

He pulled his thoughts together. "Either way," he replied, "I'm grateful for the lift. *Nein*, don't get out," he added as she made to secure the reins. "If you just give me a moment, I'll get my suitcases in the back."

He heaved the heavy valises into the back of the buggy and then climbed into the seat beside Emma. He saw her gaze flick to the scar on his cheek, but she said nothing. Instead, with an ease born of experience, she directed the horse back across the highway and toward town.

"Was your trip long?" she asked in a clear attempt at small talk.

"*Ja*. Very long. I'm glad to be here." He hesitated. "For a while, I thought I was in the wrong place. It was nice to hear horse hooves at last."

"*Ja*, Uncle Samuel got tied up in a meeting or he would have been here an hour ago. My aunt is watching my daughter."

"Are we going far?"

"*You* aren't," she replied with a smile. "I'm dropping you off at a boardinghouse in town. It's run by some people from our church. But my aunt and uncle live about three miles beyond the edge of the town. That's where most of us live."

"Is this the only Amish church in Montana?"

"*Nein*, I think there are about five others scattered widely, but we're the newest. A few years ago, the church bought up a huge ranch that was on the market and has been parceling it out as farms ever since. It's nice because we're all clustered together on our own but fairly close to town."

"Pierce seems like a pretty place."

"It is. You'll like it here. See that?"

Thomas looked over to where she was pointing and saw a storefront with a broad front porch stocked with flowers in buckets of water for sale. *"Ja?"*

"That's Yoder's Mercantile. I'm temporarily working there three days a week. My uncle said that's where you'll be working, too, *ja*?"

"It is." He peered closely at the store and decided he liked the look of it. It had a comfortable, settled air. There was even a hitching post for buggies across two of the angled parking slots. "And it looks like the town is making accommodations for us."

"You mean the parking spaces for buggies? *Ja*, it's true. I think half the time the townspeople view us as quaint players in costumes, but they've been very welcoming."

It was as he'd suspected. Emma was very outspoken and high-spirited.

"And do you see that small vacant store next to the mercantile?"

Thomas saw the boarded-up windows of a small retail space. It had a Realtor's sign affixed to the door. *"Ja?"*

"I plan to rent that and open my own business."

"Really! That's wonderful. What kind of business?" He was impressed. For such a young woman, she seemed like quite a go-getter.

"Soaps." She smiled with satisfaction. "I earn money

in a number of different ways, but my handmade soaps are such *gut* sellers at the mercantile that I'm certain I can expand into my own store."

Thomas's business sense went into alert mode. "What else will you sell besides soap?"

"That's it. Just soap."

He could hardly offer any financial advice to a stranger on such short acquaintance. Instead, he settled with a mild warning. "It seems like a very small town to support such a specialized business."

She tossed her head. "I know what I'm doing. My soaps are the best in town and regularly sell out. You'll be doing the bookkeeping at the Yoder's store, so you'll see what I mean."

"As you say." Despite the financial warning bells, he chuckled.

"What's so funny?" She quirked a glance at him.

He decided to be truthful. "If you really want to know, I was hoping your husband appreciates how high-spirited you are. It's refreshing."

He saw her lips firm. "I'm widowed," she said shortly.

He winced, conscious of putting his foot in his mouth. "I'm so sorry…"

"Don't be. I'm not." She gave a defiant toss of her head.

Thomas was shocked to his core. Was Emma a merry widow? On the surface, it certainly seemed that way.

Her personal issues were none of his business. He didn't want to get off on the wrong foot in his new community.

"It still must not have been easy for you," he said quietly. "That's all I'll say about it."

From the corner of his eye, he saw her stare straight ahead, as if she hadn't expected a comment like that.

"Danke," she murmured at last.

* * *

Emma wondered what was wrong with this new fellow Thomas. His dark blue eyes shifted away from a direct gaze. He kept his shoulders just the slightest bit hunched. Even his straight brown hair looked subdued somehow. All the Amish men she'd known throughout her life had been a blend of humble and confident. Thomas Kemp seemed beaten down somehow. A small maternal part of her felt sorry for him, but she refused to analyze it. Thomas Kemp's problems were not hers. She had enough problems of her own.

The reins in her calloused hands felt good. She was familiar with horses, familiar with driving both buggies and wagons. She had fought hard for her confidence and, as a result, she was good at almost everything she did, whether it was making soap or canning vegetables or gardening or housecleaning or endless other bits and pieces she did to earn a living and support her daughter. Now, she planned to be good at running her own store.

The only thing she wasn't good at was choosing someone to marry.

Thomas's quiet words of sympathy about losing her husband struck her harder than she'd expected. She stared ahead at the town's traffic, automatically guiding the horse through intersections as she reflected on how relieved she was to be free of the burden of matrimony. The only good thing to come of that disastrous relationship was her three-year-old daughter, Hannah.

Thomas stayed quiet beside her. She appreciated his tact on the issue of her personal life.

She directed the horse down a side street where a large two-story building dominated one block. "This is the boardinghouse," she said, pointing to a sign outside the establishment that read Miller's Lodging. "It's kind of a catchall business. They rent rooms, and the *Englisch* often stay here as a kind of motel. They sometimes host weddings and things like that. So many of our church members don't yet have homes large enough for big functions, so we often use the Millers' building."

"I see." Thomas scanned the structure. "It's a handsome place."

"*Ja*, they fixed it up nicely. The Millers are lovely people. It's family run. Matthew, the middle son, is mostly in charge, but Millers come and go, doing whatever needs to be done." She pulled the horse to a stop in front of a hitching post for Amish visitors. "*Komm*, I'll help you get settled in."

She climbed out of the buggy as Thomas leaped down and started hauling his suitcases from the back—all four. She seized two as he took the others.

"These are heavy," he exclaimed. "I can take them, don't worry—"

"I'm not fragile," she retorted. The suitcases were heavy, yes, but she refused to admit it. "Let's go."

His face took on a bemused expression, but he merely shrugged and walked into the boardinghouse lobby with his luggage. She followed.

The inside of the structure had typical Amish style— clean lines, lots of wood, simple furniture. The front desk was deserted, but Emma smartly tapped the desk bell and, within seconds, Matthew Miller poked his head out of the doorway leading to the back living quarters. "*Guder nammidaag*, Emma." His blue eyes crinkled over his clean-shaven face.

"*Guder nammidaag*. Matthew, this is Thomas Kemp. He just arrived. He'll be doing the bookkeeping at Yoder's Mercantile."

"*Ach, ja.* The bishop mentioned you." Matthew reached over and shook Thomas's hand. *"Welkom."*

"*Danke.* It was a long trip. I'm glad to be here."

"I have a nice sunny room for you on the second floor, unless you'd prefer the ground level?"

"Second floor is fine."

Emma stood back as Thomas signed in. When the paperwork was complete, Matthew came around the desk and relieved Emma of the two suitcases she'd carried in.

When it became clear Matthew would settle in his new guest and she had no reason to linger, Thomas turned to her. "*Vielen dank* for picking me up at the bus stop. If you could tell your uncle I'd like a meeting with him at some point, I'd be grateful." His expression and tone indicated an eagerness to please.

She remembered her uncle's request. "I'm sorry, I meant to tell you Uncle Samuel asked if you could meet with him after the church service this Sunday."

"*Ja*, I'd be happy to."

"Well." She dawdled a moment but knew it was time for her to go. "I'll see you at the store later this week." With that awkward statement, she nodded and left the establishment.

She felt thoughtful as she unhitched the horse and swung into the buggy seat. Thomas was an interesting soul. Handsome, yes, but quiet and subdued. She got the impression he carried the heavy weight of past problems on his shoulders.

If she was honest with herself, she had to admit there was something about Thomas that piqued her interest, but she refused to analyze or dwell on it. She had no intention of ever getting involved with a man again. Of course, if her aunt and uncle knew about that promise, they would thoroughly disagree with it.

But Emma had not traveled all the way from her old hometown in Indiana as a single mother to be burdened once again with another *hutband*. One was enough. Once was enough.

By the time she pulled up in front of her aunt and uncle's barn, she had managed to put Thomas out of her head.

Uncle Samuel came out to greet her and put away the buggy. The older man was tall and lanky with a wispy beard and an air of authority that came from being the bishop. "*Vielen dank* for picking up the new man," he told her. "How was he?"

"Fine." She climbed down from the buggy. "Seems like a strange fellow. Very subdued and quiet, but nice enough. I pointed out the Yoder's store and took him to the boardinghouse. He said meeting with you after church this Sunday would be fine."

"*Gut. Nein*, don't bother with the horse, I'll take care of him. I'm sure Hannah wants to see you."

Emma smiled at the thought of her daughter's eagerness. Leaving the horse to her uncle, she twitched her apron straight and headed for the house.

"*Mamm! Mamm!*" The brown-haired child had flour on her apron and cheeks from the cookies she was making with her grandaunt. She stood on the kitchen chair and held up her arms.

"There's my *liebling*." Emma caught up her daughter and twirled her around in a hug, making the child giggle. "I see you're helping Aunt Lois make cookies. What a big girl you're getting to be."

She would die for this child. Hannah meant more to Emma than anything else in the world. She was determined to be the toddler's mother *and* father.

"Everything turn out all right?" inquired her aunt,

pressing a fork neatly across the peanut butter cookies on the sheet before her. Lois Beiler was short and plump, and her gray hair was tucked neatly under her *kapp.*

"*Ja.* No problems. I dropped him off at the boarding-house, and Matthew took him right in with all his luggage." Holding Hannah in one arm, Emma snagged a baked cookie from the cooling rack. She took a bite and then broke off a piece for Hannah. "I was just telling Uncle Samuel he's kind of an odd duck, though. Very quiet and subdued. I'm not sure what to make of him."

"Well, if he's been traveling by bus all the way from Indiana, I imagine he's exhausted."

"*Ja,* I'm sure you're right. What do you say, little one?" Emma said to her daughter. "I have some soap to wrap up, now that it's cured. We can bring it to sell in the Yoder's store tomorrow. Do you want to help me pick some herbs in the morning? We can bring those too."

"*Ja! Ja!*" The child bounced in Emma's arms.

"Take some cookies," ordered Lois. "It's not like your uncle and I can eat them all ourselves."

Emma packed the treats in a small basket, kissed her aunt on the cheek, took Hannah's hand and started for home.

"Home" was a small and charming little cottage, formerly a barn, located a short distance from her aunt and uncle's home. Before Emma had arrived in Montana, fleeing the memories of a husband she'd never wanted, the church carpenters had insulated it against cold winters and then outfitted the structure as a small house. It was too small for the typically large Amish family, but was perfect for Emma and her daughter. Emma had planted Virginia creeper around the porch rails and along the fencing, and she maintained a large vegetable garden and a small flock of chickens. Her pride and joy was the herb beds.

"Come, *liebling*, I need to wrap the last batch of soap. It's completely cured now. You can also help me decide what herbs to bring to the store tomorrow, *ja*?"

"Ja, Mamm!" Hannah skipped ahead toward the garden, her face serious as she bent to examine spearmint with a knowledgeable air. She pinched off a leaf and took a deep sniff. "Like candy," she said.

Emma chuckled. Her little daughter loved plants and gardening as much as she did.

She settled into her usual afternoon habits—wrapping the cured bars of soap, feeding and watering the chickens, gathering eggs, preparing dinner. All the while, her daughter tagged along at her heels. Emma involved the child with as many things as she was capable, determined to pass on to her daughter the competency she would need as she grew up.

The work was routine, but for once, Emma's thoughts weren't focused on the tasks at hand. She kept thinking of Thomas. It wasn't like her to give two thoughts to a man, but there was something about him that grabbed her attention—a mix of shyness, poignancy and perhaps the heaviness of something weighing on him. Threaded through her thoughts was a vein of annoyance at his polite doubts about her business plans.

She caught herself and gave a small shrug of dismissal. She didn't owe proof of business success to Thomas or anyone else, except perhaps the bank she hoped would lend her the startup funds.

Six months with her husband had been six months too many. She was done with men. Done forever.

Chapter Two

Thomas got ready for his first day of work at Yoder's Mercantile. He hoped the store would be the first of many clients for the bookkeeping business he wanted to establish, something he could expand until it was capable of supporting a family. After witnessing the sheer joy his older brother, Joseph, had found with his new bride, Thomas knew eventually he, too, wanted to become a family man.

But it would take a special woman to overlook his past. His mind flickered to Emma Fisher and then darted away. She was out of his league. Not worth thinking about.

Sliding the suspender straps over his shoulders, he gave his hair a perfunctory combing, grabbed his hat, said a prayer and left his cheery little second-floor room in the boardinghouse.

"First day of work, *ja*?" inquired Matthew Miller as Thomas came down the stairs. The hotelier stood behind the front desk making notations in a ledger amid a sprawl of paperwork.

"*Ja.* I—I hope they like me."

"I can't imagine they won't. The Yoders are fine people. The store is a big success, so they're delighted to get a bookkeeper in, especially one who understands Plain businesses." Matthew gestured toward his ledger. "In fact, let me know if you want any more work."

"Are you serious?" Thomas approached the desk with its messy collection of receipts, bills, tabs and other paperwork. "Do you need a bookkeeper, too?"

"Not full time, but I wouldn't mind some help," admitted Matthew. "The Yoders have so much going on all the time, so a full-time bookkeeper makes sense. I just don't like dealing with paperwork. Are you interested?"

"Ja!" Thomas hoped his voice didn't sound too eager. "I mean, give me some time to settle in and get myself established, but I hope to form a bookkeeping business and will be looking for clients. Not preparing taxes, but day-to-day maintenance of business operations."

"Count me in." Matthew gave him a cheeky grin. "In fact, the sooner I can shove this paperwork at you, the better."

"You're on." Thomas returned the grin and then plopped his straw hat on his head. "Meanwhile, I'm off to meet the Yoders."

"You'll do great."

Warmed by Matthew's enthusiasm—and the thought of another potential customer—Thomas stepped out into the warm August morning and headed for the mercantile. The town had the subdued bustle of a new workday. Cars angled into parking slots, pedestrians strode the sidewalks with purpose and the front doors of a few stores were being unlocked to greet the day. He heard a buggy or two clip-clopping in the distance, but it seemed most church members avoided the main street since it wasn't wide enough to comfortably accommodate horse-drawn vehicles.

Yoder's Mercantile was just a short three blocks from

the boardinghouse. Thomas paused in front of the building, gathering more details since he'd only gotten a brief impression yesterday while driving with Emma. The store had a broad front porch covered by an awning, and there were steps in front and a ramp at one end. Buckets of bright and beautiful blooms crowded one side of the porch. The store windows displayed a range of merchandise—crafts, fabrics, antiques, quilts. It seemed like a welcoming place, including for a former jailbird like him.

He mounted the steps, took a deep breath and swung open the door.

The smell of baking and coffee assailed his nose, causing his stomach to growl since he'd skipped breakfast. The worn wooden floors beneath his feet were scrubbed and clean. Glancing around, he took in the general mix of dry goods with a few select groceries, local produce and a dairy case. A deserted coffee area was separated by a low half wall with children's playthings inside.

"Good morning." A feminine voice spoke from nearby. "May I help you?"

He turned and saw a plump, grandmotherly woman in Amish attire. She glanced with some uncertainty at his straw hat and then at the scar on his cheek. She'd spoken in English.

He replied in German. "*Guder mariye.* Are you Mabel Yoder?"

"*Ja.*" Recognition dawned on her face. "Are you Thomas Kemp?"

"*Ja.*"

"*Welkom.*" Her face wreathed in smiles, Mabel shook his hand and then called, "Abe! Abraham! The new bookkeeper is here."

A man emerged from a back room, wiping his hands

on a canvas apron. "*Guder mariye*. So nice to meet you." Thomas found his hand pumped again.

"*Komm*, I'll show you around the store," offered Abe. "We're open but don't normally get the morning crowd for another hour or so. Then the coffee shop portion will be very busy."

"Is it just you and Mabel working this place?" Thomas glanced around at the various different departments crammed into the medium-sized store and wondered how two people could handle it.

"*Nein*, all our adult children work here with us, and often our older grandkids as well. We have a daughter who's about ready to have a baby, so we've hired another woman temporarily." Abe chuckled. "For the most part, it's very much a family-run business. The town has been very *gut* to us, very supportive."

"Once they got over the novelty of Amish *kapps*," added Mabel with a smile.

Thomas followed Abe around the store as the older man showed him the bakery section, the coffee shop, the selection of dry goods. "We're something of an outlet for many in the church who have surplus produce to sell," explained Abe, "or those who have specialty items such as quilts or soap, things like that."

"I can see why a bookkeeper is needed," remarked Thomas. "This is a lot to juggle."

"*Ja*, especially since we have to keep track of incoming inventory as church members drop things here to sell. The business aspect is fairly routine by now. It's just a matter of keeping up with everything, but it takes time. Frankly, it will be a relief to have someone dedicated to handling it."

"Well, I'm anxious to get to work. My hope is I can get everything streamlined to the point where it doesn't take as much time." Privately, he also hoped for enough time to work with other clients as well, such as Matthew at the boardinghouse.

Abe showed him into a small back office with a generous window overlooking an alley. It was outfitted with a comfortable chair, an old-fashioned oak desk, file cabinets, and a number of ledgers and notepads.

"Show me how you've done things up to this point," said Thomas.

For the next hour, Abe explained his bookkeeping system. Right away, Thomas could see some areas that could be improved, but he decided to wait before suggesting them.

"All this make sense?" concluded Abe at last.

"Absolutely." Thomas gave his new boss a broad smile. "Believe it or not, I actually enjoy working with numbers."

"Better you than me." Abe gave an exaggerated shudder and then smiled back. "And don't hesitate to take as many breaks as you need. I know it's tough sitting at a desk for hours at a time. Stroll the store, look over our inventory…"

Just then Thomas's stomach gave an embarrassingly loud rumble. He clapped two hands across his midsection and gave Abe a sheepish grin.

"Have you had breakfast?" the older man asked.

"Nein…"

"Then don't do a thing more until you have a cup of coffee and some of the scones our daughter makes. They're exquisite."

Thomas accepted the offer but vowed to eat something before work next time. He didn't want to come across as a freeloader.

He followed Abe to the bakery section, selected a

modest two scones, poured a cup of coffee and then re-treated back to his cave to eat at his desk. The store was picking up with customers and Thomas preferred to be invisible.

He bowed his head for a silent prayer before tucking in to the delicious scones. The prayer was a prayer of gratitude—praise for the God who had pulled him out of the abyss before it was too late; gratitude for this new church community where he could get a fresh start; and a request for guidance that he would be able to work hard and prove himself worthy.

Feeling more at peace, he tackled the ledgers and note-books in front of him. For the next couple of hours, he was busy.

He stopped to stretch for a moment. Standing, he arched his back and then stood looking out the window at the alleyway that was scattered with empty cardboard boxes and a few wooden pallets. Inexplicably, he found his mind going back to the woman he'd met yesterday. Emma Fisher.

Thinking of her caused his shoulders to droop a bit. He realized he was somewhat in awe of her—her air of shining purity, her confidence, her poise. She seemed to have it all. She was a cherished niece of the bishop and a hardworking member of the church. It was an in-timidating combination—except for that curious bit of rebellion he'd seen when they'd spoken about her de-ceased husband.

He realized he would never have the slightest chance of courting someone like that. Not with his past hang-ing over his head. Yes, it was best if he put all thoughts of Emma Fisher out of his head.

A small noise in his office doorway caused him to turn around. He froze. As if conjuring up a vision, there she was, right in front of him, holding the hand of a small child.

She gave him a cool smile. *"Guder mariye."*

He felt a pulse beat in his throat. He kept his hands still by his sides. She was even more beautiful than he remembered. "Ah, *guder mariye.*"

Why was she here? And why had she specifically stopped by his office?

The child next to her caught his attention. She was delicate with large brown eyes like her mother's, and brown hair neatly tucked under a miniature *kapp*. He felt an arrow pierce his heart. What he wouldn't give for a child like that of his own.

Emma's heart gave a little flop at the expression of stark longing on Thomas's face when he looked at her daughter. She knew with sure instinct that this was a man who wanted children. Why wasn't he married? Why had he launched himself across the country to settle in a new place? How did he get that scar on his cheek? There was a mystery here.

A sudden thought occurred to her. Had he lost a child? That might account for that aura of sadness and the piercing look of longing on his face.

"I was told by Abe Yoder to let you know what items I brought today to sell at the store," she said, more to snap him out of his child-induced trance than anything else.

He dragged his eyes away from Hannah and spoke to her. *"Ja,* sure." He gave a little shake of his head, turned to open a file drawer and pulled out a folder. "This is the form the Yoders use. I might make some changes to it in the future, but my understanding is everyone's used to it."

"Ja. Danke." She took the form.

"What is it you brought in?"

"Soap. Remember, I'm famous for my soap." She gave him a dry smile. "Plus, I have some bundles of fresh herbs from my garden." His hair was a little squashed from the hat that now hung on a wall hook, and his dark blue eyes looked like holes into his soul.

"So, you have many accomplishments." He gave a thin smile that didn't reach his eyes. "And I only have one." He gestured toward the clutter of paperwork on his desk.

Emma was startled. What an unusual thing to say, especially since every Amish man she knew was an experienced carpenter. "I'm sure that's not the case," she contradicted. "I'll bet you transform when you have a hammer in your hands."

He faced relaxed into a more genuine smile. "*Ja*, you're right. I like building things. I helped my brother and his new wife build a home this past summer."

Hannah, who up to this point had been holding Emma's hand, suddenly jerked free and toddled toward Thomas. Without a word, she raised her arms to be picked up.

Emma's mouth dropped open. Hannah never approached strangers, much less asked to be picked up. Why would the child do that?

Thomas looked at her for permission. She snapped her mouth shut and gave a nod. He reached down and hoisted the toddler into his arms.

"Hi. Hi," said the child with a smile.

"Hi there, little one." Thomas gently booped the girl on the nose. "And what's your name?"

"Nanna."

"Hannah," Emma interpreted with a smile. "This is wild. I've never seen her walk up to a perfect stranger like that."

"She's sweet. I've always wanted kids." Thomas

looked at the child in his arms as she toyed with his suspender strap.

Emma ventured to say, "You've never been married?"

"*Nein.* No one wanted… I mean *nein.* I've never been married."

Yes, there was some sort of mystery there. Perhaps he'd lost a wife. Perhaps he wasn't able to have kids. Whatever it was, she could hardly inquire.

"So…are you planning on staying at the boardinghouse for the long run? Because if you get tired of living in just one room, I'm sure my aunt and uncle can help you find a place to live."

"I don't know. I haven't even been here twenty-four hours yet." He gave her a wry smile over the top of Hannah's head. "The boardinghouse is certainly a convenient distance from here, so it's easy to walk. Since I don't have a horse and buggy, it's probably best I stay in town. Where are church services normally held?"

"Out in the settlement. Right now the only people with a home big enough to host is the Stoltzfus family. I'm sure the Millers or Yoders can give you a ride," she replied.

"*Ja.*" He paused. "There's so much I don't have. Most men my age already have a business, a home. A family. Even a horse and buggy. I have a lot of catching up to do."

She burned to ask more but instead settled for a neutral question. "How old are you?"

"Twenty-five."

"That's hardly old." She smiled. "You have time."

"*Ja*, I suppose." He paused. "So you brought soap to sell. And you want to open a store selling it as well. What kind do you make?"

Clearly, he was anxious to avoid personal topics. Emma accepted the change of subject. "Tallow soap, mostly. There's a butcher in town who keeps beef fat scraps for me. I render the tallow and use it to make my soap. Today's batch is pine soap. We don't have a shortage of pines around here so…"

"Pine needs!" Hannah gave a little jump in Thomas's arms. "I help with pine needs!"

"She helps me collect the pine needles," explained Emma. She smiled at her daughter. "She's a wonderful little helper. She helped pick all the herbs we bundled up and brought in today too."

"Mint." The child wiggled. "Like candy."

Thomas chuckled. "*Ja*, like candy. You sound like a *gut* girl." With reluctance, he placed her back on the floor.

But rather than toddle over to Emma, Hannah tugged on Thomas's pant leg. "Mint," she demanded. "Come see mint."

"Now, *liebling*, Mr. Thomas needs to get back to work," said Emma.

The child looked crestfallen, but she returned to her mother.

"I can come look at your mint," Thomas said. "I was just taking a break anyway."

"Mint!" Breaking into a smile, Hannah dashed out the office door.

"Hannah, get back here." Emma darted after her impulsive daughter and caught the child by the shoulder before she could barrel into the increasing numbers of customers in the store. Swinging the toddler into her arms, she scolded her daughter. "You know better than to run away."

"Show mint." Hannah pouted.

Emma looked over toward Thomas. "And so you shall. But the Yoders have customers, and it's not polite to dash in between people, *ja*?"

"Ja, Mamm." Looking chastised, Hannah squirmed to get down.

Emma set her daughter on the floor. With greater solemnity, the child went over toward Thomas, took his hand and tugged him along.

"I guess I'm going to go look at mint," he commented with a twinkle in his eye.

"Ja, I guess so." Chuckling, she followed as Hannah led the man to the produce section of the floor, where the bundles of herbs tied with twine were already on display.

"Mint," declared Hannah, pointing. Emma was pleased at the child's restraint. It had taken a lot of training to prevent the toddler from touching the freshly washed cuttings. "And basil. Sage. Rosm."

"That's rosemary," Emma interpreted.

"Wow. The kid knows her herbs," observed Thomas.

"She's grown up with them," explained Emma. "Spearmint is her favorite. She says it's like candy."

"Candy!" Hannah grinned.

Thomas smiled. "This little one is endearing."

"Ja, she is." Emma could hardly explain to a virtual stranger the fierce love she had for her daughter. She knew almost all women experienced the same emotion, but somehow she still felt overwhelmed by it. Maybe because it was just the two of them, but she felt highly protective of her daughter, like a mama bear.

It had surprised her that the child had walked up to a stranger and asked to be picked up. For the first time since her husband had died while she was pregnant with Hannah, Emma wondered if she was doing her daughter a disservice by raising her without a father. But Emma refused, absolutely refused, to remarry solely for that purpose. Hannah had lots of father figures in her life, starting with her Uncle Samuel. And she had never before shown any particular interest in men.

So why was Hannah drawn to Thomas? What did the child see in the shy, hesitant bookkeeper?

Emma examined him as he gravely followed the child's lisping explanations about the herb bundles. He had the typical muscles of an experienced carpenter, even though his primary job was bookkeeping. He was good-looking in a generic sort of way. He was, in short, absolutely unexceptional…except Hannah seemed fascinated by him. It was a puzzle.

"*Komm, liebling*, let's get some milk and butter and then go home. I told Aunt Lois I'd help her clean house this afternoon."

"*Ja, Mamm.*" The child turned from the herb display.

"You clean houses too?" Thomas asked.

"*Ja.* My aunt is slowing down a bit, so I help her out. Cleaning house is the least I can do since she watches Hannah while I work here. I also help some other older people with housekeeping, as long as they let me bring Hannah with me. It's just another bit of income for us."

"You sound resourceful."

"I've had to be." She thinned her lips. "It's what widows do, *ja*?"

"*Ja*, I suppose. Well, I'd better get back to work. I don't want the Yoders to think I'm slacking on my first day on the job."

She nodded. "I'll see you Sunday at church."

"*Ja.*" He crouched down and again touched Hannah gently on the nose. "See you on Sunday, *ja*? You can bring me some mint."

"*Ja!*" Hannah threw herself against Thomas and his arms automatically wrapped around the child in a hug. Then he released her and stood up. Emma was startled to see moisture in his eyes. He turned to go back into his office.

Emma took Hannah's hand and led the child outside to where her horse was hitched to the buggy. She felt a little stunned at the whole interaction with Thomas.

And part of her was determined to find out his secret.

Chapter Three

On Sunday morning, Thomas accepted a lift to the Sabbath services from Matthew Miller, the boardinghouse proprietor.

Matthew was in a chatty mood, describing how his family came to Montana in search of less expensive farmland. "So I decided to follow them," he concluded, guiding the horse at a sedate trot toward the home where the service would be held. "When they saw the building in town, they knew it would be a *gut* family investment. They lived there while they fixed it up as a boardinghouse, but *Daed* missed his cows, so they ended up back on the farm."

Thomas responded politely to Matthew's conversation, but his mind was elsewhere. He was heading to his very first church service in the new town. The people he had met so far—Matthew, the Yoders, the bishop, Emma— had all been very welcoming, but Thomas was aware his acceptance here hinged on the bishop's discretion about keeping his past a secret. It was an uneasy feeling. He had yet to meet the church leader in person.

He wanted to return to his roots. He wanted a normal life, not a life of petty thuggery. He wanted a family. He wanted respect. And above all, he wanted to be baptized—a decision that must be unanimous within the church community. He felt like he was walking a tight-rope.

"But no wife yet," said Matthew.

Thomas brought his mind back to his companion's conversation. "You're not courting anyone?"

"There's no one here to court." Matthew winked. "But I might be able to convince a certain young lady at my old church in Ohio to travel this way. We'll see."

The other man seemed cheerfully unfazed by his marital status. As for "no one here to court," Thomas wondered if that included Emma Fisher. She was a beautiful and eligible young woman. Why weren't there men lining up to court her?

Matthew continued to talk about the area, pointing out landmarks and chattering about who lived where as the horse trotted serenely toward the farm where the church service was being held. Thomas closed his eyes a moment, drew in a deep breath and put his worries into *Gott*'s hands. He breathed in the warm August air and focused on the birdsong and sweet smell of grass and pine.

"Who is hosting the Sabbath service this week?" he inquired of Matthew.

"The Stoltzfus family," replied Matthew, expertly guiding the horse around a corner. "Here in Montana, everyone is still building up their farms, so we don't have a lot of homes large enough to host. The exception is Amos and June Stoltzfus's home, so they've become the default place to hold services. They're very good-natured about it. Everyone pitches in to help clean up before and after, so they're not overwhelmed with work." He grinned. "In fact, June Stoltzfus once said it's an easy way to get the whole farm tidied up twice a month."

Thomas chuckled. "What a *gut* attitude."

"*Ja*, they're *gut* people. How are you liking it here so far?"

"Very much." Thomas spoke truthfully. "I like the town, I like the scenery and I like the Yoders. I haven't met many others, but the bishop said he would formally introduce me today after the service, so I guess I'll be meeting others soon enough."

"*Ja*, and I think you'll enjoy getting to know everyone. We're a close-knit group."

Soon enough Matthew pulled his rig into the crowded yard of the Stoltzfus farm. Thomas helped unhitch the horse before awkwardly filing toward the barn where the service was to be held. He sidled toward the men's side and took a seat alone near the back.

He saw Emma seated across the aisle of benches next to a plump older woman. Little Hannah was nestled in her mother's lap. Thomas looked at the pair and his throat threatened to close up. Seeing the women sitting together made him realize how much he wanted a family of his own.

Would he ever be able to find a woman willing to overlook his past? Or was he unworthy of a family?

More and more people entered the barn and took seats, but there was little by way of greetings. Fellowship happened after the service, not before. Thomas returned the polite nods and smiles of the unknown men who seated themselves around him, but no one introduced himself.

The bishop stood up to begin and Thomas saw the man who held his future in his hands. The older man was lanky and had a wispy beard, but he projected an air of quiet authority. Somehow, Thomas was comforted. His impression of the church leader was that he was a fair man.

The service proceeded like most church ceremonies. There were hymns, an introductory sermon, prayers, scripture readings, the main sermon given by the bishop, testimonies and closing prayers. And then came the moment Thomas had both anticipated and dreaded. Bishop Beiler stood to give announcements regarding church business.

"And we would like to welcome a newcomer to our settlement. Thomas Kemp," said the bishop. Thomas stood briefly, nodded his head and then dropped back onto the bench. "Thomas is working as bookkeeper for the Yoder's store in town. Please welcome him after the service."

The Sabbath service concluded with a closing hymn and then the dismissal, during which people filed out according to age and status. Thomas rather dreaded the subsequent meal and mingling. He prayed no one would mention his facial scar.

He needn't have worried. *"Welkom!"* said an older man, extending a hand to clasp. "I'm Isaac Lapp."

Another man reached for his hand. "I'm Jonathan Lambright."

"I'm Noah Graber," yet another man greeted.

Men young and old crowded around him, shaking hands and clapping him on the shoulder. Thomas knew he would never remember everyone right away, but he smiled and thanked them. When pressed, he explained briefly he had come from Indiana, but he didn't volunteer much beyond that. His heart was warmed. Everyone seemed genuinely happy to have him within their midst, and he had to remind himself that no one was a mind reader. No one had any idea of his past or the crime he committed when he was younger. He vowed to stay worthy of their acceptance.

Abe Yoder, his boss, wandered over. "Awkward to be the new guy, ain't so?"

Thomas smiled in relief. "*Ja*. How did you guess?"

"I've been in your shoes. *Komm*, why don't you eat with us?" Abe gestured toward a picnic table under the shade of a large ponderosa pine.

"*Danke…*" He trailed off as he saw Bishop Beiler approach. "I'll join you shortly," he told Abe.

"*Ja*, sure." The older man patted Thomas on the shoulder. "The bishop is a *gut* man," he murmured. "Don't be nervous."

Thomas was warmed by his boss's encouragement. He turned toward the bishop and held out his hand. "*Guder mariye.*"

"*Guder mariye.* It's so nice to meet you at last." The bishop's handshake was firm. "I'm sorry I haven't had a chance to meet with you before now. Are you still interested in coming over this afternoon?"

"*Ja*, sure. I was planning on it."

"*Gut.* Then enjoy your lunch and we can have an uninterrupted conversation later on." With a bright smile, the bishop turned to join another group.

Before Thomas could move toward the table with Abe Yoder, he suddenly felt his leg being grabbed by a small pair of hands.

"Hi! Hi!" Little Hannah Fisher tugged at his trouser leg, her face wreathed in smiles. Thomas smiled back and bent to pick her up. "Well, hello! Are you by yourself? Where's your *mamm*?"

"Hi! Hi!" she repeated, all smiles.

Thomas knew Emma would be worried if Hannah had gone missing, so he started walking around, looking for her. He saw her near the house where large tables laden with food had been set up. She had a worried look on her face as she scanned the area.

"Looking for someone?" he inquired, walking up to her.

"Hannah!" Emma reached over to take her daughter. "Naughty child, where have you been?"

The toddler pointed. "Mr. Thomas."

"*Ja*, I see. But you can't just run away from me when you see someone. Understand, *liebling*?"

"*Ja, Mamm.*" The child looked a bit shamefaced, but nowhere near as guilty as she should.

Emma looked over the girl's head at Thomas. "Sorry about that. She just disappeared on me."

"I don't know if she came looking for me or just happened to see me. Either way, I didn't mind. She's a sweet kid." He hooked his fingers through his suspenders and backed up a step or two. "Well, the Yoders invited me to eat with them." He touched the brim of his hat and moved away.

He stood in line before the spread of food, making awkward conversation with an older woman whose name he'd missed. He filled a plate and joined the Yoders at their picnic table.

"Ah, Thomas," said Abe. "Have you met Joshua Schrock? We're building his house next week."

"*Nein.* How do you do?" Thomas shook the man's hand. Joshua had pleasant blue eyes and a short beard.

"If you feel like swinging a hammer," Abe continued, "we're having a work party on Friday and Saturday. Are you interested?"

"*Ja*, sure." He smiled at his boss. "But it means I won't be at the store crunching numbers."

"Neither will I. The numbers can wait. It's more important to get a house built."

"*Ja*, I'd like that, then." He closed his eyes, said a fast blessing over the food and then took a bite of potato salad. "All last summer, I helped my brother and his new wife build a new home. Where are you staying now, if you have no house?"

"We've been camping in a barn at the Millers' place," said Joshua. "As you can imagine, my wife is anxious to have a proper roof over her head. We have three *kinner*. Almost four."

"Who is the foreman of the project?" asked Thomas.

"A fellow named Adam Chupp," explained Abe. "He's probably the best carpenter we have. He has a business building log cabins."

"Is that what we're building next week, then?"

"*Nein*, my wife prefers a house made of boards, not logs." Joshua's eyes twinkled. "And I'm not prepared to argue with a pregnant woman."

Thomas felt a moment's envy of the other man's obvious domestic happiness, but he let it pass. He was celebrating inside. Carpentry projects always brought out male camaraderie. He was pleased to be asked, pleased to know he had the skills to keep up with the other men. It was another chance to prove himself.

It seemed he might fit in well here—as long as no one found out about his past.

Emma made sure to keep Hannah at her side during the rest of the mealtime. She didn't want the child to wander off again and make herself a nuisance.

She ate with her aunt and uncle, as well as a couple of the graybeards who were friends with her uncle. She listened to the conversation without saying much. Her ears perked up when one of the elders mentioned Thomas. "He comes from Indiana, *ja*?"

"Ja," replied her uncle. He forked some casserole into his mouth, chewed and swallowed before continuing. "His brother is Amish and owns a store out there. Thomas is not baptized yet, but wants to be. Because he spent time in the *Englisch* world, he knows how to use computers. He computerized the entire inventory and bookkeeping for his brother's store, simply because it was too big a place to keep the books by hand any longer. The Yoders mentioned they were looking for a bookkeeper just at the time his letter asking to migrate came across my desk. It seemed like a *gut* match."

"Do the Yoders want to computerize?" asked Lois in surprise.

"Nein, but Thomas is skilled in bookkeeping by hand," Samuel replied.

"I wonder why he wanted to migrate?" mused one of the other men.

"Why did any of us want to migrate?" countered the bishop. "A fresh start. More affordable property. New horizons."

"It is nice to have elbow room," agreed the other man. "So much less crowded than in Ohio."

Mabel Yoder came over, a glass of lemonade in hand, and plopped herself across the picnic table from Emma and her Aunt Lois. She wiped her forehead with a handkerchief. *"Ach*, it's getting to be a warm day." She pocketed the cloth. "We're organizing the food for next week's house building for the Schrock family," she told the women. "Will you be there?"

"Ja, of course. How many people are expected?" inquired Lois.

"At least thirty. Our new man, Thomas, will be there too. He has carpentry experience. Abe said it's more important to build homes than crunch numbers, so he'll be working both Friday and Saturday." She chuckled.

"How is he working out as your bookkeeper?" inquired Lois.

"Wonderfully." Mabel smiled. "I don't know how he does as much as he does so quickly. He's amazingly efficient, and it's already made a difference in how smoothly the store runs."

"That's *gut*, then." Lois gave Emma a lightning glance from the corner of her eyes.

Emma noticed the glance and tensed. Was her aunt trying to match her up with Thomas?

"My only worry," continued Mabel, "is he's so efficient, we may not have enough work to keep him busy full time."

This last remark caught the attention of the bishop. "You're running out of work for Thomas already?" he asked.

"*Nein*, not at all. But we may not have enough work to keep him on full time." Mabel took a sip of her lemonade. "He mentioned he might be interested in starting his own bookkeeping business in addition to working for us. That's fine with Abe and me. He said if he does that, our store would be his first and biggest customer. He wants to focus on Plain businesses—not to do taxes, but just keep books."

"I have a meeting with him this afternoon," remarked the bishop. "I'll ask him about it. He seems to have a *gut* head for business, so I don't think he'll have trouble getting all the clients he wants."

"What about you, Emma?" asked her aunt. "Maybe he can help you with getting your soap business started."

Where did this line of questioning come from? Emma shrugged with what she hoped was nonchalance. "I think

I've got everything I need already," she replied. "I just need to make an appointment with a banker." A part of her had an uneasy feeling she was being pushed toward Thomas in a way she wasn't prepared for.

She had spent so long—since Hannah's birth—steeling herself toward independence that she no longer questioned her desire to stay single. Marrying her husband had been a mistake, though she would never admit getting pregnant with Hannah was anything to regret. But she never wanted to put herself in that position again. Within her church, marriage was an irrevocable commitment, even when the causes—such as an out-of-wedlock pregnancy—were less than ideal.

For the first time in a long time, Emma's mind went back to her husband, Simeon. What had she ever seen in him? Why had she compromised her future with a man whose personality had turned out to be the polar opposite of hers? It's not like they had been childhood sweethearts. Instead, he was just an excuse for some teenage rebellion on her part. In retrospect, she should have known better than to risk her future with an unbaptized man. She would be miserable right now if he were still alive.

Simeon had been handsome, fun, high-spirited and unorthodox. She had found his streak of rebelliousness attractive. Unfortunately, that fractious streak hadn't translated into suitable husband material. She'd learned that the hard way.

"Is that possible, Emma?"

Emma snapped out of her reverie. Her Aunt Lois had been speaking to her. "I'm sorry, I was thinking of something else. What did you say?"

"I said that your uncle wants to know if you can bring some of our garden produce to the Yoder's store tomorrow. We're getting overwhelmed with blueberries, and Mabel says they don't have any in stock at the moment."

"*Ja*, sure." She'd agreed automatically but, after a moment, the request sank in and took on a deeper nuance toward matchmaking, which annoyed her. "But I'll be working Wednesday and Thursday. Can they wait a couple of days until my workday?"

"I want everything to be as fresh as possible," countered Lois. "But, *ja*, I suppose they can wait."

"If you have any corn or green beans in your garden, we could use some to sell," added Mabel.

"*Ja*, I have plenty—" Emma began.

"And be sure to get them inventoried so we make sure you get paid."

Get them inventoried. That meant interacting with Thomas. Emma looked at the store owner with narrowed eyes. Yes, Lois and Mabel were certainly conspiring to push her in the direction of Thomas. She almost smiled. They meant well, but it wasn't going to work.

She hadn't discussed her intention to remain single with anyone. It wasn't normal in the church to reject matrimony, and she knew it would not be comprehensible to the older generation why she'd made that choice. It was just easier to avoid the issue altogether.

She wondered if anyone ever asked why she was so determined to work at whatever she could to earn money. It wasn't just the obvious need to support herself and her daughter. It was also so she would not be forced to marry for financial reasons. That's why she was so determined to see her soap business succeed.

Aunt Lois and Mabel might push her to interact with Thomas, but they could hardly do more than that. She wasn't a pregnant and vulnerable teen anymore. There was nothing to compel her to marry anyone. Anyone at all.

The meal broke up as everyone became sated with food. The women started gathering dishes and children. The men began hitching horses. The older boys and younger men started loading benches into the special wagon designed to carry and store the seats between church services. Emma let Hannah go play with some children her age, keeping an eye on the youngster so she wouldn't dart away again.

To her irritation, as Thomas walked by carrying a bench, Hannah darted over and started trotting next to him. "Hi! Hi!"

"Hannah, get back here," scolded Emma. "Mr. Thomas has his hands full."

Thomas chuckled, put the bench down and picked up the toddler, who gave him a big smile.

Emma walked over, clucking in annoyance at her little daughter's new obsession. "I'm sorry," she said. "I don't know what's gotten into her."

"It's all right. I like kids, so I don't mind." He transferred the child into her arms. "I just don't want her hurt when I'm carrying something big, like a bench."

"She knows better." Emma gave Hannah a little bounce against her hip. "Don't you, *liebling*? You can't bother people when they're carrying heavy things."

"Ja, Mamm." The child had an unrepentant look on her face. For a moment, her expression reminded Emma of her deceased husband. It left her with a lingering sense of unease.

Later, she walked back to her cabin, pulling Hannah in a wagon. Last summer, at her request, her Uncle Samuel had kitted the wagon with extra-large wheels so the little vehicle was easier to pull along gravel roads. Hannah was too big to carry for long distances now, especially if

Emma had other things to transport, and the specialized wagon suited her needs.

As she walked, she considered her daughter's personality. It was easy to think she could raise her child without a father, but could she really disregard the fact that half of the toddler's genes came from a man she would just as soon forget?

Was it enough to raise Hannah within the church community but without a father in the home? Emma had no desire to remarry. But what did Hannah need?

She stared ahead at the gravel road shimmering in the warm August sun and recalled the few months of her marriage. She'd been pregnant with a baby and trying to cope with a man so different than her. She had been miserable and unhappy. When Simeon was killed in a car accident, she had mourned him in a proper fashion, all while fighting off the guilty sense of relief that she was free of him.

Yes, she had no problem being single. But what about Hannah? What did Hannah need?

Emma didn't like the direction her thoughts were leading.

Chapter Four

When the after-church meal wound down, Thomas saw the bishop walking toward him. He knew what was coming: his formal interview with the church leader. Discreetly, he wiped the palms of his hands on his thighs.

"Won't you come back to our place in the buggy?" asked the bishop. "It will save you a walk."

"*Danke*, I appreciate that," Thomas replied with a calm he did not feel. "Let me just tell Matthew that I won't need a ride home."

He relayed the message to his landlord and then headed toward the buggy area where the bishop was helping the plump older woman he'd seen earlier.

"Thomas, have you met my wife, Lois?" the older man said.

"*Nein*. How do you do?" Thomas reached over to shake the woman's hand. She had graying hair and twinkling eyes.

"Are you okay riding in back?" she inquired.

"*Ja*, of course." He decided to joke back. "It's not like I could ask you to ride back there."

She laughed outright, and Thomas was comforted.

Lois dominated the conversation for most of the ride

home, asking about his impressions of the town and his job. To Thomas, it seemed she was deliberately keeping the atmosphere neutral and nonpersonal, and he was careful to respond in kind.

Within a few minutes, the bishop pulled the buggy into a small landholding with an old barn that had been renovated into a cozy home. Traditionally, older people lived in a *daadi haus* behind an adult child's farmhouse, but Abe had told him the Amish settlement was still working on housing for its current and incoming members, and so unorthodox solutions were being used. It was also why, Abe had said, he hoped Thomas would be willing to join in some of the home-raising and barn-raising events as needed.

The Beilers' little home was surrounded by the normal trappings of a small farm. There was a large garden, some young fruit trees, a chicken yard and what looked like the accoutrements for pigs.

When the bishop pulled the buggy to a stop before the small barn, Thomas leaped from the back and dashed around to assist Lois down.

"Danke," she replied, her eyes sparkling. She laid a hand in his as she climbed with stiff grace from the conveyance. "Come inside while Samuel stables the horse."

He followed her into the small and tidy home. Thomas barely noticed details since he was focused on making sure he appeared both respectful and deferential.

"Would you like some lemonade?" inquired Lois.

"Ja, danke," replied Thomas. He wasn't thirsty, but he thought it might be rude to refuse.

He followed the small figure into the kitchen. Lois removed a pitcher from the icebox and poured him a glass just as the bishop came in.

"I'll take one, too, *lieb*," the older man said.

When the bishop had his beverage in hand, he gestured toward Thomas. "My office is this way."

Thomas trailed behind the church leader into a small, sparsely furnished room with a desk, a file cabinet and two comfortable guest chairs. A padded basket on the desktop held a beautiful calico cat, which raised its head and blinked at him.

"Please, sit down." Samuel motioned to a seat. He closed the office door and took his own chair behind the desk.

"Beautiful cat," commented Thomas, giving the animal a brief pat before seating himself.

"*Ja*, she's my favorite pet." The bishop leaned back and looked narrowly at Thomas. "I'm glad we have a chance to talk," the older man began. "How are you doing? Have you forgiven yourself yet?"

Startled that the church leader would cut to the chase so quickly, Thomas was silent a moment. "No," he admitted at last. "I haven't. I made such a mess of my life. I feel… I feel like I've just been reborn, that I've climbed out of a black pit. My entire life has been something of a bad dream from which I'm just emerging."

The bishop picked up a long, typewritten, multipage letter from his desk. Thomas recognized it as the full confession he had made to the bishop during the early days of inquiring whether there was room for him in the new Montana settlement. "Obviously, I've read your letter—multiple times, I might add—but I'd like you to tell me everything. This is all in confidence, I might add. No one need know about it."

Thomas had expected this line of questioning, so he complied. He began with his childhood and explained the boyish rebellion that had caused him to fight against the church teachings and the rules of the *Ordnung*. He explained the jealousy he'd felt for his older brother, Joseph, who was always the "good" kid. "It was like the devil was sitting on my shoulder, urging me to do worse and worse things," he admitted. "I didn't fight it. I embraced it. My parents never stopped worrying about me. Neither did my sister. My brother, I think, just gave up on me."

"Did you ever get counseled by any church elders?" inquired the bishop.

"*Ja*, they tried. They tried many times, and every time, I paid no attention. I'm certain that if I hadn't left the church during my *rumspringa*, I would have been kicked out. But my behavior simply got worse and worse—drunk driving, petty theft, thuggery. I had to cool my heels in jail a couple times."

He avoided the look of deep sympathy in the bishop's eyes. Instead, Thomas focused his gaze on the cat. "The low point is when my parents were killed in a buggy accident." He wiped away a tear. "I denied it was my behavior at the time, but I know my father was distracted by my latest escapade and inattentively drove the buggy into traffic. It's not an easy thing to be even indirectly responsible for the deaths of one's own parents."

The bishop made a sound of sympathy in his throat, but he didn't say anything.

Thomas plunged on. "My sister, Miriam, is the only one who stuck by me all these years. It's not that she condoned my behavior—far from it—but she kept bailing me out of jail and giving me money when I needed it. She left the Amish to become a nurse, and I'm ashamed to say I was a leech on her tender conscience, even following her when she took a job at a hospital in Chaffinch, Indiana, the town I came from. By sheer coincidence, my brother also settled in that town, since he was buying a store. And…and that's when it all came to a head."

"When you were accused of involuntary manslaughter, *ja*?"

"*Ja*. I was running with a gang. The absolute wrong kind of people, but they accepted me. Or so I'd thought. Then, late one night, when I was at my apartment, I walked across a courtyard to get a soda from a vending machine. By the grace of *Gott*, a closed-circuit camera caught me on film. At that same moment, the gang leader accidentally killed some poor innocent soul. He immediately fingered me as the culprit and, with my reputation, that was easy to believe. The gang leader slashed my face and then ratted on me. Next thing I knew, I was arrested and thrown in jail." He drew a deep, shuddering breath. "Miriam went to our brother, Joseph, and pleaded my case, telling him I needed money to hire an attorney who could subpoena that closed-circuit tape before it was erased. I begged him to help. I told him I would turn over a new leaf if he hired an attorney. He didn't want to do it, but he did. Then he told me it was the last time he would ever have anything to do with me if I broke my word."

"So he hired an attorney, your name was cleared and then what?"

"I kept my word." Thomas raised his chin and met the older man's eyes. "I've turned over a new leaf. I refuse to go back to what I was. I wanted to pay my brother back for the money he spent on the attorney, for the gift he gave me, but he wouldn't let me. Instead, he told me to pay it forward, that someday I'll meet someone who needs help, and that's how I can repay him. I promised to do that."

"He sounds like a *gut* man, your brother."

"He is. Oh, he is. My only goal now is to leave my past behind. To return to my church. To redeem myself. To get baptized. To start a bookkeeping business. To be a respected member of the community. And maybe, someday, to court a woman." He choked a bit. "And you, bishop, are the one giving me that opportunity. I'm more grateful than I can say."

A suspicious sheen of moisture was visible in Samuel's eyes. He nodded. "None of us walk on water, Thomas. If you're serious about changing, we'll know by your fruits. But I'm pleased to have you here, and I have every confidence you'll continue to work toward the goals you mentioned."

"Danke." Thomas gulped air. He felt better. "I'm also grateful for your discretion. As you can imagine, I don't want my background to be common knowledge."

"As the church leader, it's my position to hear the sins of many people. You can trust me to keep your confidence. Now, on to practical matters. How is your position at the Yoder's store? Are you comfortable at the boardinghouse?"

For the next half hour, Thomas talked with the bishop about the logistics of his living situation, the impressions of his first few days on the job and his hopes for establishing a bookkeeping business. He wanted to ask about the bishop's niece but refrained. It was one thing to accept a former jailbird back into the fold. It was another thing entirely to have that jailbird express interest in his pretty and available niece.

When the meeting was over, Samuel stood up and shook Thomas's hand with a firm grip.

Emerging from the bishop's house, Thomas blinked in the sunlight. He felt better, like a weight had lifted from his shoulders. He took a deep and cleansing breath. It was just like the Bible said—to confess one's sins to one another was healing. For the first time in a long time, Thomas felt more optimistic about his future.

* * *

"Would you like to pull some carrots for dinner, *liebling*?" Emma asked her daughter.

"Ja!" The child ran for the small basket a church member had recently given her. The girl treasured the gift and looked for any excuse to use it.

Emma gathered her own basket as well as a trowel and headed outside. Her vegetable garden was near the front door, well fenced against the area's resident deer population. Emma opened the gate so Hannah could slip through.

The child skipped among the raised vegetable beds. The little girl knew right where to find the carrots.

Emma paused to examine some corn for ripeness. She made a mental note to harvest the garlic. She observed that the blueberries were nearly finished with their run— she had several quarts of canned blueberry pie filling in her pantry to show for it—and she saw it was time to cut some more broccoli so the brassica would continue to sprout more heads. The ones she had earmarked for seed were ripening well.

Emma felt more at home in her garden than almost anywhere else. She could—and did—spend hours every day tending the raised beds. As often as not, Hannah was with her. The child had two beds of her very own in which she grew a mishmash of vegetables and flowers.

But today was Sunday, a day of rest. There would be no weeding, no cultivating. But picking carrots for dinner? That was hardly work.

"*Mamm*, look." Hannah's voice pierced her reverie. "Nice man."

Emma looked to where Hannah's finger pointed. Thomas Kemp was walking down the road. Her eyes widened and her stomach gave a little lurch. He must be coming from a meeting with her uncle.

Thomas seemed equally startled at seeing her. He stopped in the road for a moment and then approached the high deer netting around the garden as Hannah ran over, two carrots in her hand.

"Hi! Hi!" the child squealed.

"Hello." Thomas smiled at her. "What's that you have?"

"Carrots." Hannah poked an orange vegetable coated with dirt through the mesh of the netting. "See?"

"I do see." Thomas touched the carrot with a finger. "Are you helping your *mamm*?"

"*Ja.* Carrots for dinner." The child grinned up at the man.

Emma drew near. "*Guder nammidaag.* Did you have a meeting with my uncle?"

He seemed a little skittish. "*Ja.* He said he wanted to talk to me after church."

She nodded. "Uncle Samuel likes to do that with all new church members."

"So, you live here?" His gesture took in the garden, the cottage, the chicken coop.

"*Ja.* The house is too small for most families, but Hannah and I don't need much room."

"This is a beautiful garden."

"*Danke.*" Her eyes softened. "It's part of how I earn my living, but I love this garden. It's all mine." She bit her lip. That phrase sounded selfish.

Thomas evidently had picked up on the unusual phrasing. For the first time, she saw humor and inquisitiveness on his face. "As opposed to what?" he teased.

But it wasn't a teasing matter to her. "As opposed to sharing it with a selfish, aggressive man," she snapped.

Instantly, she regretted those words. She clapped a hand over her mouth.

The teasing expression dropped from his face and was replaced with one of sympathy. He murmured, "You've been hurt."

It wasn't common for church members to discuss emotions. Thomas making such an observation—and an accurate one at that—made her eyes burn with tears. She turned to look at Hannah. "Maybe," she muttered.

"Care to discuss it?"

Surprised, she looked at him. The offer was tantamount to a shoulder to cry on, which was a surprisingly attractive prospect. But that wasn't her way. When Hannah was born, she had vowed to stay strong, stay independent. But Thomas's gentle offer made her realize just how much was bottled up inside her. For the first time, she wondered if that was healthy.

"Nein, danke," she replied. It was all she could say.

As if feeling the moment had been too tinged with emotion, Thomas looked down at Hannah, who was still holding the two carrots. "May I see around your garden?"

"Ja, sure." Again, she was surprised. "But why?"

"Because I haven't been in nearly as many gardens as I should have over the last few years."

She raised an eyebrow and parroted his words back at him. "Care to discuss it?"

His grin nearly took her breath away. Smiling, Thomas was a very handsome man. "As the French might say, touché. And, no, I don't care to discuss it."

She grinned back, realizing they had somehow turned a corner. It seemed they both had baggage they were eager to avoid discussing. "The gate is over there. Hannah, why don't you show Mr. Thomas where the gate is?"

"Ja, Mamm." The child dropped her carrots and took off.

Emma picked up the fallen vegetables and went over to place them in her basket. She found herself pleased to show Thomas around her pride and joy.

But Hannah had absconded with the visitor. Taking him by the hand, she led him from one bed to another, lisping out the names of the plants. She could tell Thomas was both amused and impressed as he gravely listened to the child's chatter.

"Carrots," Hannah finally announced, returning to the same bed they had been digging in when he arrived. "Carrots for dinner."

"She loves carrots," supplied Emma.

"Wow." Thomas removed his straw hat and ran a hand through his straight brown hair. "The kid knows her vegetables."

"I have no option but to keep her with me whenever I'm working out here, so she's picked things up. She's worked this garden with me almost since she was born."

"This space feeds your soul, it seems."

Would he never cease to startle her? She stared at him for a moment before turning her face away. *"Ja,"* she admitted. "This garden feeds my soul. It's as easy for me to pray in a garden as it is at the church services."

"Gott hears us no matter where we are." He scrubbed a hand over his face. "I should know that better than anyone."

She smiled. "Care to discuss it?"

He laughed out loud. *"Nein.* All I'll say is *Gott ist gut."*

Yes, they had definitely turned a corner. Emma felt a tentative interest in the man, which was odd. No one had caught her eye in years, certainly not since she had fallen pregnant with Hannah out of wedlock and been compelled to marry Simeon. It was a bad match from the start, and Emma had prayed for forbearance as her dislike for her husband deepened into contempt as he began criticizing her for everything and undermining her confidence.

Her husband—unbaptized and dabbling in *Englisch* habits—had bought a car. He had also bought some alcohol. The two, as she'd learned when a police officer had come to break the news to her, didn't mix.

She had no interest in explaining any of this complicated background to Thomas. She had so many regrets, it was hard to list them all. Emma had decided she would never apologize for her mistakes. She would simply not repeat them. And one of those mistakes she refused to repeat was marrying an unsuitable man.

That was why it unnerved her to see her tiny daughter fixate on Thomas.

"Penny for your thoughts?" the man inquired.

Emma snapped out of her past. She eyed him and then gave him a neutral smile. "I don't ever reveal my thoughts," she told him. "My thoughts are my own."

"Got it." He patted Hannah on the head. "And on that note, I'll be going. *Danke* for showing me your garden. It's beautiful. *Faeriwell*, little one," he added to Hannah.

Unhurried, Thomas let himself out the gate and continued his walk down the road.

Emma stared after him. Okay, perhaps her words had sounded rude. Certainly, it seemed Thomas had thought so. She sighed. Whatever fleeting interest she might have had in Thomas, it seemed she had nipped that in the bud.

What she wasn't certain about was whether she was relieved about that or not. She was so used to holding men at arm's length that it was instinct not to respond to anyone's interest. The result was a sharp tongue that sometimes got the best of her.

"I like Mr. Thomas," said Hannah thoughtfully.

Emma glanced down and saw her little daughter was staring at his retreating figure. "I like Mr. Thomas, too, *liebling*," she admitted.

She hoped those words would not come back to bite her.

Chapter Five

Emma pushed open the door to the Yoder's store early on one of her workdays. Hannah was being cared for by Aunt Lois, and Emma knew her daughter was in safe hands. Still, Emma wasn't used to being without her child's near-constant presence and felt a bit at a loss without her.

"*Guder mariye*, Emma." Mabel Yoder was busy stocking some display shelves. "Would you mind working the bakery section today? Esther just brought over a fresh batch of goodies, which I imagine will disappear by afternoon."

"*Ja*, sure." Emma made her way toward the wonderfully scented section of the store where baked goods were sold. Esther Mast was the settlement's best pastry chef, known for her delicate tarts and delicious cupcakes. She was widowed and made a tidy living keeping the townspeople supplied with mouthwatering treats.

She passed the prominent display the Yoders had put together to showcase her soaps. The inclined wooden case had two dozen separate cubicles, each housing a stack of differently scented bars. It never failed to give her a frisson of pleasure to see her handiwork on display. She picked up one bar, inhaled the lemon scent and then returned the bar to its cubicle before making her way to the bakery department.

The store's bakery section was adjacent to the small coffee area, complete with small tables and chairs. The townspeople often lingered in the coffee area, working on laptops or chatting with friends.

Emma greeted Amos Yoder, the youngest Yoder son, who was operating the espresso machine and filling coffee orders for some early customers. She was immediately plunged into some sales of scones and muffins by customers who wanted a snack along with their coffee.

Between customers, she organized the fresh pastries and tarts in an eye-catching arrangement beneath the curved display glass. She made sure each type of pastry had a label and price.

She had learned so much since working for the Yoders, like how to arrange products to attract a customer's eye, how to properly price a product, even how to treat customers. Mabel Yoder had taught her that most *Englisch* expected an open and friendly salesperson with just a bit of demure aloofness they seemed to expect from Amish church members. Mabel herself had chuckled at the absurdity of that assessment, but Emma had found the older woman was right.

As she casually chatted with the largely *Englisch* clientele, she wondered where Thomas was. Was he in his office? Had he not arrived yet? She wasn't certain of his hours.

From the corner of her eye, she noticed two women lingering over the prominent display of her soaps the Yoders had set up. Busy in the bakery section, she couldn't go over to answer any questions, but she watched with delight as the women examined the bars, lifting them to sniff the scents and chatting between themselves over the choices. Finally, they selected several bars each and brought them to the front counter to ring up.

She smiled to herself, feeling a bit smug.

At that moment, Thomas emerged from his back office. He raised his eyebrows in an apparent question at her smile.

Reading his unspoken inquiry, she jerked her head toward where the two customers were paying for the soap. Thomas looked at the women and watched as Mabel rang up their sales. He nodded and strolled over to the bakery section.

"Nice," is all he said.

"Danke." She brushed imaginary crumbs from her apron. "And just you watch. I'll probably have to bring in more soap by tomorrow."

"I see the Yoders have given you a dedicated display. That must mean you're selling well."

"Ja, I am." This time, she didn't even try to keep the smugness from her voice. "So you see, that's why I think a store will do well."

He shrugged, a gesture that made her thin her lips. "I'm happy to see you're so confident."

She lifted her chin. *"Ja,* I am. I'm also determined. And that, Mr. Kemp, has gotten me far since I lost my husband. Excuse me," she added as another cluster of customers descended on the bakery department. "I need to get back to work."

She offered the customers her sunniest smiles, but inside, she was annoyed. Clearly, Thomas still had doubts about her abilities to start her own store. At the same time, she recognized the irrationality of such thoughts. She barely knew Thomas. Why was she concerned about his opinion?

She wasn't. Irritably, she wiped down the glass

counter, making sure it sparkled. Her husband had torn down her confidence in a few short months. It had taken her years to build it back up. She wasn't about to let the new guy disturb her hard-won convictions on how best to earn money to support herself and her child.

She stopped her fussy actions, closed her eyes and took a calming breath. It wasn't Thomas's fault that she still felt the sting from her own bad choices when she was younger. She said a prayer for tranquility and resumed her duties, determined not to shift any blame for her insecurities on the Yoders' new bookkeeper.

Yet even though Thomas had disappeared back into his office, she was conscious enough of his presence to work extra hard and demonstrate she was knowledgeable and efficient. She never knew when he might glimpse her, and she wanted to make sure she always projected an air of brisk authority.

It was particularly ironic he should reemerge from his office just as an *Englisch* man should begin flirting with her. It was a common-enough occurrence, just… annoying.

"These pastries look as good as you do," the man said, licking his lips. He looked to be in his early forties and had something of a paunch. "Are you Amish?"

"I am, *ja*." Emma gave him a frosty smile. "These pastries are made by an older woman in our church. Is there a particular one you'd care to try?"

"Which one do you recommend?" He waggled his eyebrows in an expression he probably thought was suggestive, but Emma decided it looked comically ridiculous.

"The blueberry-cheesecake tarts are always popular." Emma gestured toward the items. "As you can see, there are only two left."

"If I buy them both, would you care to join me?" He

pointed to an empty table and waggled his eyebrows again. "Something this delicious is best enjoyed with company."

Emma wanted nothing more than to laugh in his face, but she knew Mabel would not approve of rudeness toward a customer. She caught Thomas's eye and flushed, aware he was hearing the whole conversation.

"No, thank you," she told the man with icy politeness. "I'm working. Did you want one tart, or both?"

"Tart," the man muttered, his expression turning sullen. "That's what you are." He turned on his heel and stalked away.

Emma exhaled a breath as Thomas strolled over. "Does that happen a lot?" he asked in German.

"More often than you'd think," she admitted. She leaned back against the counter and wiped a bead of sweat with a corner of her apron. She eyed the man as he left the store. "Mabel warned me when I first started working here that some men look at a *kapp* as a challenge. She was right, as always."

"You handled him well."

"*Danke.* It wasn't easy. What I *really* wanted to do was… Well, never mind."

He chuckled. "It's not hard to read your mind. The guy never had a chance."

"You're right about that." Her voice was sharp. "And no one ever will, either."

He seemed a bit startled at the vehemence in her tone and she immediately regretted revealing even an inkling of her emotions. "Sorry," she muttered. "People like that always leave me shaken."

He nodded, his expression more sober. "That's understandable. What seems amusing to me must be less so to you, even if you *did* handle him well."

"Danke."

An older couple came over to the bakery section and Thomas retreated. "I'll let you get back to work," he told her.

She smiled at him and then turned her attention to the pleasant couple, but her mind buzzed. Thomas always seemed to understand her at some level, which she found disconcerting.

She worked automatically—supplying pastries to customers, wiping tables, cleaning the glass display cover—but her mind raced ahead of her industrious hands.

She was determined to focus on financial independence. Working in the Yoder's store, even temporarily, wasn't an ideal situation since she couldn't have Hannah with her. The toddler had been her shadow since birth, and Emma preferred ways to earn money that were compatible with keeping the child with her.

That's why having her own store seemed like such an ideal situation. Emma had concrete ideas how the building would be laid out. She wanted a work area in back where she could engage in manufacturing and where she could complete the more dangerous steps—such as working with lye—in a separate space. The child would have to be limited to certain areas, which was regrettable but necessary. She hoped her daughter—used to the freedom of a garden—could adapt to a more confined environment.

"So, I'll take half a dozen, please."

Emma snapped back to reality. The young woman she had been helping was smiling at her, pointing to some cupcakes in the case. Emma murmured an apology for her lapse in attention and completed the sale.

Perhaps it was time to take the concrete steps and

make her dream a reality. Perhaps it was time to make an appointment with a bank loan officer.

A teenage boy caught her attention. She stiffened. The little brat was back…

"Hey! Drop that!"

Thomas's head snapped up and he jerked out of his chair, going through the open door of his office in time to see Emma literally chasing a teenage boy through the store. The youth wore dirty clothes and a sullen expression and clutched a bag of candy to his chest. For an eerie moment, Thomas saw himself as he used to be, engaged in petty crime more for the thrill than any sense of need.

The boy evaded Emma's pursuit and dashed out the front door of the store onto the sunny street, avoiding Abe Yoder's last-second attempt to grab him. Emma pulled herself to a stop, an expression of fury on her face.

Abe Yoder huffed out a breath of annoyance. Turning, he tried to soothe Emma. "Don't let him get under your skin, Emma. It was just a bag of candy."

"But he took it practically under my nose," she fumed. "I should have seen that coming."

"Troublemaker?" Thomas inquired, joining the group.

"Ja," she spat with unusual hostility. "This is the second time he's taken something."

Abe turned to Thomas with calm resignation. "Actually, it's a lot more than his second time," he explained. "He's the town's troublemaker." Abe patted Emma on the shoulder. "He's more annoying than dangerous, Emma. He's not worth getting incensed." With admirable composure, the older man made his way back toward the cash register.

Thomas turned to the still-simmering Emma. "If Abe can be so calm about the kid, why can't you?"

"Because Abe's right," she snapped. "He's a trouble-maker. He has a history of shoplifting—not just from here, but from other stores. He's no good, that boy."

"I wonder why," he murmured almost to himself.

"Why what?" With an agitated gesture, she pushed a loosened strand of hair back under her *kapp*.

"Why he behaves the way he does. I—" He hesitated. "I used to know someone like that, and he later made a complete turnaround and became a reformed person."

"I can't see that happening with this kid," she declared. "He's irredeemable." She turned on her heel and stalked off.

Thomas stared after her, not sure whether to be bemused or alarmed. Her attitude toward the teen seemed like an overreaction. Some instinct told him the issue went deeper than just responding to a troubled boy's proclivity toward shoplifting.

But it also did not bode well for her attitude toward *him* should she ever learn about his past. He realized he craved her good opinion.

He admired Emma. He liked her little daughter. He respected her aunt and uncle. At the moment, he knew he was making a good first impression in his new church community. What he dreaded was for it to all come crashing down on his head.

And if Emma's reaction to the *Englisch* boy's misbehavior was any indication, she had no patience—no patience at all—with the kind of past he himself had just recently left behind.

He returned to his office in a thoughtful frame of mind, wondering what it might take for someone to pierce the armor Emma had wrapped herself in.

One thing was certain: that someone could not be

him. He didn't deserve anyone as good as Emma, and if the run-in with the shoplifter was any indication, Emma would probably agree with that assessment.

Chapter Six

"Let's pick *flaisch brieh*," Emma said to her daughter on Thursday morning. The green beans were coming on thick in the garden. "We'll put some aside to bring to the store in town, and we'll can the rest up. *Ja?*"

"*Ja, Mamm.* Basket?"

"Here's your basket." Emma lifted down the toddler's favorite new toy and watched as she darted out of the house.

It was a bright and beautiful morning with a promise of heat later on. Best to get any garden chores done early. She followed her daughter outdoors at a more sedate pace with two large baskets.

As she directed Hannah toward the tenderest pods to pick, she wondered if bringing in products to sell—green beans, corn, another batch of soap—was just an excuse to see Thomas on her day off.

Maybe.

The thought disturbed her at some level. She had promised herself never to get tangled up with a man ever again. And as attractive as he was, Thomas had some sort of secret about him, which didn't bode well for her peace of mind. And yet...

Hannah's little basket filled up with beans. Emma emptied it into one of the larger baskets while she also plucked the vegetable with efficient hands. In short order, the larger basket was full.

"Now let's pick some corn, *liebling*," she said. "I'll pick and you put the ears in that other basket, *ja*?"

Within fifteen minutes, the chore was done. "*Komm*, let's go fetch the wagon to carry the baskets," she told Hannah. "You can ride in it, too, since we have to take it with us to Uncle Samuel and Aunt Lois's."

She loaded the vegetables and her daughter into the wagon and set off for her aunt and uncle's home a short distance away. Her aunt was elbow-deep in blueberry bushes, a bucket at her feet.

"There's my little one." Lois waded out of the garden and caught up her grandniece in an embrace. "I have some beautiful blueberries for you to bring to town."

Emma looked at her aunt's harvest and gave a low whistle. "Your bushes are more productive than mine."

"*Ja*, this is a good year for them." Lois put the toddler down with a small grunt. "I should know better than to pick her up," she muttered.

"Is it your back again?" Emma looked at her aunt with concern.

"*Ja*. I don't like to admit I'm getting older, but my back tells me otherwise." Her aunt leaned slowly backward, stretching. "I'd be grateful if you could do some house-cleaning for me sometime this week, though."

"*Ja*, sure." It was a common request. Cleaning houses for older church members was another source of Emma's regular income, but Emma never charged her aunt and uncle since her aunt watched Hannah while Emma worked at the store. "Meanwhile, if I could use the horse and buggy, it would be easier to take these to town than to walk all that way with Hannah."

"*Ja*, your uncle is in back. See if he can hitch it up for you. I'll watch this little one."

Half an hour later, Emma thanked her uncle, touched the reins to the horse's back and took off for town with Hannah next to her on the seat. The back was loaded with corn and green beans, blueberries, and two dozen jars of Lois's homemade raspberry jam.

She found a free slot at the hitching post in front of Yoder's Mercantile. Emma climbed from the buggy, tied up the horse and lifted down her daughter.

"Stay close," she warned. "There are cars driving up and down this street. I don't want you getting hit."

Emma retrieved one basket of blueberries, took Hannah by the hand and led her into the store. A bell jingled overhead as she pushed the door open.

"*Guder mariye*, Emma," said Mabel, writing on a notepad next to the cash register. "Are those your aunt's blueberries?"

"*Ja.* I have lots more in the buggy, along with jam and green beans and corn. Can Abe help me unload?"

"Abe is out on an errand. Hang on, I'll see if Thomas can help. Meanwhile, I'll watch this little one."

Scooping up Hannah in her arms, Mabel moved toward the back of the store. Emma stared after her for a couple seconds before heading out to the buggy. Yes, unquestionably, Mabel and Lois were collaborating as matchmakers.

She had already off-loaded the baskets of produce and a box with jars of jam as Thomas came out of the store. He looked amused. "I heard you need a hand," he remarked.

Was he aware of the older women's swirls of intrigue? Emma wasn't about to ask.

"Ja," she replied, handing him the heavy box of jams. "Lots of things from Aunt Lois as well as from my garden."

They brought everything into the store and piled it on the counter. Hannah leaned out of Mabel's arms, reaching for Thomas. With a chuckle, he placed the last basket on the floor and pulled the child into his arms. "Are you being a *gut* girl for your *mamm* today?" he inquired.

"Picked beans!" the toddler announced triumphantly.

"What? No corn?" Thomas's eyes twinkled as he nodded his head toward the heaping basket.

"Ja, corn too. I helped." The child's face shone.

Mabel unloaded the produce and weighed it, making notes on a pad on a clipboard as she did so. "Twenty pounds *flaisch brieh*, Emma Fisher," she muttered. "Twenty-four pints of jam, Lois Beiler."

Watching her, Emma realized why the Yoders needed a bookkeeper. They had to keep track of endless inventory coming in as well as being sold, and that was undoubtedly just the beginning.

"Mabel, I can do that," suggested Thomas gently.

The older woman stopped, pen poised in hand. She looked shell-shocked for a moment, then she grinned. "I forget," she admitted. "It's such a habit. *Ja,* if you could take this over, I'd be grateful."

"Liebling, time for you to go back to your *mamm,"* he told Hannah and placed the child on the floor.

Mabel handed him the clipboard with the inventory sheet just as an *Englisch* customer came into the store. She left Thomas and Emma together as she went to see if the man needed help.

"I see why they hired you," Emma ventured. She

reached down to pick up Hannah. "It must be a tremendous task to keep everything documented."

"*Ja.* I don't know how they did it up to this point. But the store my brother owns in Indiana is bigger, and my sister-in-law kept the books by hand for years. They reluctantly admitted they had to computerize, but they weren't happy about it."

"Are you going to computerize this store?" asked Emma in surprise. Such modern solutions were not un-heard of, but they were discouraged.

"*Nein*, they haven't asked me to," Thomas replied. "And, frankly, I don't see the need. Once I get a more streamlined system set up, I should be able to maintain the books without a problem, and probably on a part-time basis." He reached out and touched Hannah lightly on her nose, causing the child to smile. "Are you heading home now?"

"Almost. First, I'm stopping at the bank to make an appointment with the loan officer."

Surprised, Thomas jerked his gaze to hers. "Now? About leasing the space next door?"

She elevated her eyebrows. "*Ja*, now. And, *ja*, about leasing the space next door. Why?"

He rubbed his chin. "Emma, do you have a business plan already written?"

"N-no," she stuttered. "What's that?"

He was alarmed. "It's the first thing the loan officer will ask to see. It's a detailed document that defines your business goals and how you plan to achieve them. Think of it like a written road map. If you've never put together a business plan, you'd better have one in place before you see the loan officer."

He saw a quiver of panic on her face. "Is it something that can be done quickly?"

"It depends on how much paperwork you already have assembled."

Her shoulders relaxed a bit. "I have all the paperwork I need. I think." She paused. "Can you help me assemble this business plan?"

"*Ja*, I'd be happy to. But a lot depends on when you end up getting your appointment with the loan officer."

"Why don't I request an appointment for, say, next week?"

"If you already have all the paperwork assembled, then, *ja*, that should be plenty of time. A business plan has a fairly structured format, so it will just be a matter of plugging things in."

"*Gut.*" She smiled. "It seems you're more concerned than I am, Thomas. Believe me, I've assembled all the materials to bring in to a loan officer already. If it's as structured as you say, then putting it into this format won't take long. W-would you like to come to dinner tonight at my place? Then I can show you everything I have."

At the slight hesitation in her voice, his gaze sharpened, but her expression remained guileless. "*Ja, danke,*" he replied, clamping down on any eagerness in his voice. "What time?"

"Six o'clock?"

"Six o'clock, then." She looked at the child in her arms. "Say goodbye to Mr. Thomas, *liebling*. We need to go to the bank and then get the horse and buggy back to Uncle Samuel."

"Bye-bye, Mr. Thomas!" lisped the child.

He touched the toddler's cheek. "*Faeriwell*, little one. I'll see you tonight."

After Emma and Hannah left, Thomas had to resist the urge to pump his fist in the air. Dinner with Emma! He knew she was out of his league, yet she appeared to like him.

Could he ever hope to earn her favor in the future? It was a goal worth striving for.

Feeling optimistic, he took the inventory sheets he had filled in for the produce and logged them into the store's ledger. His fingers worked automatically but his mind wandered.

Together with Matthew Miller and the Yoders, he had the start of his own business. And if he launched his own business, maybe—just maybe—he might someday be in a position to acquire the usual trappings of Amish adulthood: a place of his own, a means of transportation and a solid financial foundation to offer a wife.

He was so far behind other men his age. While they had progressed up the chain of respectable milestones in life, he'd been busy running with thugs, causing mischief and being framed for involuntary manslaughter. He had a lot of catching up to do.

Would he ever be in a position to court a woman? Would any woman be willing to overlook his past? The thought of Emma ever finding out about his background filled him with apprehension.

Abe Yoder bustled into his office clutching a sheaf of papers. "I've got more inventory sheets for you," said the older man, placing the documents on the desk. "Freshly cut flowers from that *Englisch* lady on the other side of town, some more pastries from Esther Mast and ten quarts of fresh milk from Ephraim King."

"I'll get them logged in right now." He quirked his boss a smile. "Did all this paperwork fall on you before I got here?"

"*Ja*, mostly me. Though, of course, Mabel did some too. Our *kinner* who often work here never got into the bookkeeping aspect."

"It seems a lot of people don't like the numbers part of a business."

"Is it true you're interested in starting a stand-alone bookkeeping business?"

"*Ja*," replied Thomas. "Matthew Miller expressed an interest in using my services. I wonder how many other Plain businesses in the settlement would welcome the thought of me doing their books?"

"Probably more than you think. Word will get around, just you watch."

"I just wish I had some means of getting around besides walking," Thomas remarked. "That way, it would be easier to visit people's businesses, especially those run on farms."

"Why don't you get yourself a bicycle?"

Thomas blinked, then slapped his forehead. "Why didn't I think of that?"

"We have a bicycle in the back room. It's got a luggage rack on the back and everything. You're welcome to use it whenever you like, until you get your own."

"*Danke.* I might borrow it tonight, then. I promised Emma I'd help her pull together a business plan before her meeting with the bank loan officer. She invited me to her place to look over the paperwork."

The older man raised his eyebrows and Thomas read the conclusion on his face as easily as if he'd spoken his theory out loud. "Did she?"

He raised a hand. "Just a business plan, that's all. Don't read too much into it."

Abe grinned. "I won't. But she's something of an

enigma, that one. Very proud, or maybe I should say standoffish. She has a stubborn, independent streak."

"Not too stubborn and independent to ask for help with her business, though."

"So it would seem." Abe turned to leave the office. "I'll go fetch the bicycle and leave it just inside the storeroom door."

"Danke." Thomas hesitated a moment as an idea occurred to him. "Abe, may I take a break for about half an hour? It occurs to me I should go to the library and check out a book on writing business plans. It might be helpful for Emma to have a concrete reference."

"Don't bother. I have a book in my office you can use. My son bought it when he was thinking of starting a business back in Ohio, but then he decided to work for us here in Montana. Hang on, I'll get it."

While Abe was searching for the volume, Thomas pushed his hands through his hair. Already, he could see the rumors starting that he and Emma were courting. While an enormous part of him would be grateful for the opportunity to do just that, he had two major blows against him. He had nothing to offer a wife and child, and she wouldn't look twice at him once she learned his background.

He thought it over and came to a miserable conclusion. At some point, if Emma continued to show interest, he would have to tell her about his past. It was only fair.

But not yet. Not yet.

Abe returned with the book and Thomas flipped through it. It was a guide for beginning businesses and couldn't be better for a novice such as Emma. "Perfect," he pronounced. "You don't mind if I leave it with Emma?"

"Nein, it's fine. She can keep it as long as she needs."

"*Danke*, Abe."

"Don't forget," the older man reminded him, "we're all pitching in on building the Schrock house tomorrow."

"I'll be there."

That evening, after his workday was complete, he took the borrowed bicycle and went back to the boardinghouse. He combed his hair and made sure his appearance was neat. Then he grinned to himself. If he wasn't careful, even he would consider this courting behavior.

Except it wasn't. It couldn't be. He wasn't right for a woman like Emma. Not yet. Maybe not ever.

Tonight's dinner was merely to write a business plan. He frowned. He had a sinking feeling there would be nothing "merely" about it. He wondered just how thoroughly Emma had thought through her determination to open a specialized store. He had a sneaking suspicion tonight's tutorial was going to be a bit more eye-opening than Emma expected.

But better to find out now than fail later. If she actually borrowed money, opened her store and then witnessed its colossal failure, it would be far more devastating— and expensive—than if she understood ahead of time her goal was unrealistic.

He couldn't stand by and watch her court financial disaster by starting a business that was doomed to fail. If she followed through with her plan, she risked ending up deeply in debt, something that could ruin her young life.

But she was stubborn and determined. While these were some of the qualities he admired about her, he was uneasily aware there was a point where determination crossed into foolishness.

There was little he could do except present the financial reality of her situation. If, as she'd indicated, she had all the paperwork and documentation necessary to pull together a stellar business plan, then great. His job would be to help her pull it all together into a professional presentation.

But if, as he suspected, the exercise of pulling together a business plan revealed large gaping holes in her financial dreams, he would be the instrument of bad news. A situation he didn't relish.

However, he knew it was better to give her bad news now than to offer encouragement and see her fail later.

With that grim thought, he plopped his hat on his head, picked up the borrowed book and left the boardinghouse to head toward Emma's home.

Chapter Seven

Riding the bike felt good after a day sitting at a desk. Thomas inhaled the sweet smells of pine and earth. A warm breeze caressed his face. The late sun was behind him.

Emma and Hannah were working in the garden as he rode up. *"Gut'n owed."*

Emma smiled. *"Gut'n owed.* Where did you get the bicycle?"

"Abe Yoder loaned it to me. I don't know why I didn't think of this sooner. I'm going to get one of my own, since I don't have a horse or buggy yet."

"Ja, gut idea."

Hannah had plastered herself to the garden fence. "Hi! Hi!"

"Hi, little one." Thomas leaned the bicycle against a tree, fished out a handkerchief and mopped his forehead. Then he fetched the borrowed book from the bicycle's basket. Hannah trotted along the inside of the garden fence, following him as he walked toward the cabin. Emma met him at the gate.

"Dinner first, then paperwork," she suggested. "Everything should be cooked."

The scent assailed him even before he hit the doorway. "It smells delicious," he said with utter truth. Home-cooked meals were a rarity for him and he realized how much he craved them.

Emma's home was small and welcoming. One long room had a kitchen at one side and a living room on the other, furnished with a braided rag rug and worn but comfortable furniture. Children's toys and books were in one corner. A short hallway in the back presumably led toward bedrooms and bathroom.

The kitchen was painted in soothing tones of cream and sage, and there was a large and battered wooden table in the center. "I do a lot of work at this table," said Emma. "Bundling herbs, preparing vegetables for canning or selling, making soap, that kind of thing. I bought it at a thrift store in town when I first came to Montana."

"Nice." Thomas sniffed the air and wished like anything this little home was his. Hannah tugged as his trouser leg and then held up her arms. He hoisted the child into his arms and, for just a moment, he pretended she was his daughter and that Emma was his wife. It was a piercingly sweet thought, and highly unrealistic.

Emma took hot pads and removed a casserole from the oven, which she set on a trivet on the table. Thomas saw the dish was rich with broccoli and onions and had a crust of breadcrumbs on the top. His mouth watered.

Emma set a salad and some fresh bread with soft homemade butter next to the casserole dish and then lifted Hannah onto a booster seat and tucked a bib under her chin. "Sit down," she ordered Thomas. "Don't be shy."

Thomas sat. The room was silent for a moment as the two adults said a blessing. Thomas was delighted to see little Hannah imitate her elders and squint her eyes closed, though he doubted she understood the meaning.

"Are you hungry?" Emma asked conversationally as she began spooning casserole onto plates.

"Actually, yes," he admitted. "And this smells so delicious, I'm trying not to be rude by grabbing the plate."

She chuckled as she handed him his portion. "Help yourself to salad and bread. Aunt Lois made the butter."

"It's been ages since I had a home-cooked meal," he admitted. He took a bite of the casserole and closed his eyes for a moment in bliss. "The restaurant I usually go to in town is *gut*, but not this *gut*."

Emma forked up a bite of salad. "You should get married."

He was surprised at her direct comment. "I've thought about it," he said cautiously. "But right now I have nothing I can offer a wife. That's why I'm eager to grow my bookkeeping business. I don't want to impose on the Yoders too much by doing work for other clients on company time, so I'll probably be doing the extra work out of my room at the boardinghouse. I might have to get an actual office. One day I'll buy a piece of land and build a house."

"It seems you're settling in very well." Emma smiled at him. "So, whatever you left behind stays behind, *ja*?"

He was startled. *"Ja,"* he said slowly. Anxious to change the subject, he shifted to her business goals. "Where do you make your soap?" he asked. "Do you do it all in this small kitchen, or do you have another place you use?"

"Here," she said. She waved vaguely with her fork. "I tend to render the tallow outside, though, since it's a smelly process. Uncle Samuel set me up with a propane burner outside."

"How is soap made?"

"You don't know?" She looked surprised.

"Nein. I remember my mother making soap, but it

was never anything I was involved in." He didn't want to admit his mother had died when he was sixteen.

Emma launched into an abbreviated chemistry lesson involving fats and lye and water and scents. Thomas listened, impressed. She knew her stuff, no question.

"How many bars do you make in a week?" he inquired.

"Well, it depends on how many other things I have going on," she replied. "But I tend to make large batches of a single type of soap at a time—say, four dozen bars of lemon soap, or pine soap, or whatever. It takes just one day to make the batch, though I let the bars cure for several weeks. And rendering the tallow is a separate job. I render a large amount about once a month. That's my least-favorite part. Are you finished eating? *Komm*, I'll show you my storage room."

She rose from the table and lifted Hannah off her booster seat. Thomas left his napkin neatly by his plate and stood to follow her.

She led the way into the back area of the house. To one side, he glimpsed a Spartan bedroom with a colorful quilt on the bed and a child's bed tucked in the corner. He averted his eyes and followed her as she opened a closed door into a second bedroom.

He stopped on the threshold as wonderful smells assailed him, a strong combination of scents. The walls were lined top to bottom with shelves stacked with different-colored bars of soap, all neatly labeled.

"Wow," he breathed. There were hundreds of bars. "I can see why you think you have enough to stock a store."

"Ja." She sounded pleased. She entered the room and began pointing. "I have each type separated, and I try to date each batch so I know how long they've been curing. The longer it cures, the harder the soap and the longer it will last."

"How did you learn all this?" He picked up a bar of lemon soap and breathed in. Next to him, little Hannah imitated his actions and picked up a bar, giving it an exaggerated sniff.

"Oh, just one of those hobbies I picked up when I was a teenager. It quickly became a passion. It wasn't until I started selling some through the Yoder's store that I realized the commercial possibility. That's when I started ramping up my inventory."

"Well." He replaced the bar of soap. "The commercial possibility is why I'm here. Are you ready to tackle writing a business plan?"

"*Ja*, sure. Perhaps you could read Hannah a story while I clear the table?"

"I'd be happy to." Thomas was pleased at the thought. He crouched down by the toddler. "What's your favorite story?"

"This!" The child darted out of the storage room toward a bookcase in the living room where she extracted a thin volume.

Thomas seated himself in a comfortable chair, pulled Hannah onto his lap and proceeded to read to the child all about an ugly duckling who became a swan. Meanwhile, Emma cleared the table, her movements neat and efficient.

It was all Thomas could do not to become maudlin over the scene. This domestic harmony was something he'd missed growing up—solely, he knew, because of his own rebellious actions. His regret about causing his parents so much pain and anguish knew no bounds.

Now here was a moment he wanted to preserve forever—a child snuggling on his lap, listening to him read; a woman who had just fed him the first home-

cooked meal he'd had in weeks. He realized how desperately he wanted this for himself.

"Ready when you are," Emma said as the story concluded.

"Up you go, little one." Thomas set Hannah on the
floor and gave her the storybook. "Your *mamm* and I
have some paperwork to do."

Emma heaved a crate of paperwork onto the kitchen
table as Thomas retrieved the book on loan from Abe
Yoder. He seated himself at table.

"Okay, let's start by going through the basic components," he began. "When you go see the banker, this is
what you'll hand him. Forget any supporting documents
you may have." He waved a hand at her crate of paperwork. "It can all be distilled down into a few pages, and
he'll be able to tell at a glance whether you're a good
prospect for a loan or not."

"Got it." Emma's focus was intense.

He opened the book to some pages he'd tagged earlier.
"Every business plan has components in common. The
categories are executive summary, company description,
objective statement, business structure, product description, sales and marketing plan, financial analysis, and
timeline." He saw dawning panic on her face and added
hastily, "Don't worry, many of these categories require
not much more than a paragraph."

"I didn't even understand half the words you said," she
confessed. He heard a slight tremor in her voice. "Business structure? Financial analysis? What are those?"

"That's what this book is for," he assured her. "We'll
get you through this, Emma. Trust me."

Emma tried not to panic at the new terminology Thomas
was throwing at her. "I honestly had no idea it would be so

complicated to ask for a loan to start a business," she confessed. "I thought if I showed up with a crate full of sales
receipts from the Yoder's store, the banker could see how
well I was selling."

"Where did you get that idea?" Thomas asked gently.

She didn't think this was the time or place to confess
the idea was entirely her own. "Never mind," she muttered. She clamped down on the feelings of inadequacy,
the same feelings her deceased husband had triggered
and even cultivated in his quest to batter her emotions.
She bit her lip. "What do we do now?"

"Now we address these points one by one." Thomas
took up a pen and paper. "Let's start with the executive
summary. It's not nearly as intimidating as it sounds,
trust me. It's just your mission statement that should list
your goal. The idea is to be as positive and optimistic
as possible. Your goal is to sell handcrafted soaps in a
wide range of fragrances through a stand-alone store."
He scribbled some notes. "Does that sound right?"

"Ja." She relaxed. He was right. The verbiage was
probably just overblown jargon required by the financial industry.

Thomas went over several other points of the plan
and, after spirited discussion, he copied down more material. Company description, objective statement, business structure, product description… Those were fairly
straightforward, and Emma's confidence surged again.
So far, this business plan was merely solidifying the ideas
she already had in her head.

"Next comes the toughest part," said Thomas. "That's
the sales and marketing plan." He read out loud from the
book. "'The marketing and sales section of your business
plan outlines the marketing strategies and sales channels
for your business. For a small business, these plans may

include local advertisements, stores, websites and retail distributors.'"

"I don't see how much harder that part is," she observed. "I plan to sell at my store."

"That's all?"

"*Ja*, that's all. What else could I do?"

He eyed her with what seemed like sympathy. "Just a warning, I don't know that the loan officer will consider that an adequate marketing plan."

"Why not?" She knew she sounded defensive. "Every store in Pierce operates like that. Why would mine be any different?"

"Because you have a specialty product, and no matter how much soap the Yoders sell on your behalf, it doesn't constitute a huge amount of money. In other words, if you were to launch a solo business, could you sell enough soap to pay the lease on the store, cover insurance and utilities, and still repay the bank for the loan? That's what the loan officer wants to know."

The panic returned, churning up her stomach. "But how would I know how much money I'll make until I make it?"

"That's where the financial analysis comes in." Thomas ran a finger over some text in the book and read out loud. "'A financial analysis provides the current income, revenue and profit-and-loss statements. Investors, partners and lenders use this analysis to assess the stability and potential of the business before providing funds and loans.'" He emphasized the last line again. "That's what the loan officer is doing when looking at your plan—analyzing the stability and potential of the business before handing over a loan."

"But I haven't started the business yet," she almost wailed. She saw her daughter freeze and stare at her open-mouthed from where she sat in the corner of the room occupied with some toys. Emma tried to master her rising fears. "How can I provide all this information for a business when I haven't even started the business yet?"

"Well, no one—not even a loan officer—expects you to turn a profit from day one," Thomas replied in a soothing tone. "That's the last part of the business plan—the projected timeline. It creates a realistic timeline of when you will show a profit, based not just on calculations, but also by looking at similar businesses and seeing how they're going."

She stared at a bare spot on the table while her mind churned with anxiety. "There are no other similar businesses in town," she croaked. "How am I supposed to provide that?"

"There are probably stores in larger cities that can get by with selling nothing but soap," explained Thomas. "But that's the critical distinction. They're in larger cities. Pierce is small and isolated, and there are only so many people in town who can—or would want to—buy handmade soap. Most are probably fine buying commercial soap from the grocery store. And *that's* what you're competing against."

"So what should I do?"

"If you want to make this business succeed, you'll have to do one of two things. Either sell something else besides soap—in which case you'll be competing with the Yoders' already well-established store—or expand your marketing by aggressively advertising beyond the boundaries of Pierce. Advertising is a large part of the budget for any retail business, and with good reason. How can people know you have a product if you haven't advertised it? This could mean building a website and selling soaps online as well."

Too many issues beyond her comprehension made Emma feel like she was being buffeted and battered. Website? Advertising? Online sales? There was so much she didn't know!

Unless… She narrowed her eyes and looked at Thomas. "You're trying to discourage me."

"*Ja*, I am," he admitted, closing the book with a soft plop. "Or rather, I'm trying to warn you. I'm not making this up to frighten you, Emma. You need to understand the seriousness of what you're undertaking if you really want to open a store. It's not just the fun of decorating a space and sitting behind a counter all day. Instead, it's juggling the many aspects of running a retail establishment while at the same time having a banker breathing down your neck, asking for repayment for the loan he gave you." He shook his head. "In short, you're likely to be too great a financial risk for the bank."

"Pessimist," she snapped.

"No, *realist*." He leaned back in the chair. "I urge you to reconsider your plan, because the last thing you should do is put yourself in debt for a business venture that isn't likely to succeed." He nodded toward Hannah, who had resumed playing quietly in the corner. "You don't want to jeopardize your future, or hers, by borrowing money with no way to repay it."

He paused and added, "That store is likely vacant for a reason. Another business before you thought they could make it, and they failed. We don't even have a tourist base here. My brother's store back in Indiana was literally a tourist destination all by itself, and busloads of tourists would pass through town to see the quaint and charming Amish." His voice descended into sarcasm. "But regardless of the motive, the customer base was there. Here in Pierce, it's not. We're too remote."

Her internal alarm solidified into stubbornness. "And if I go ahead with my plans anyway?"

"Then I wish you every success," he replied simply. "Ultimately, it's none of my business. But I have to ask… why are you so insistent? You're an enterprising woman and you earn money in a wide variety of ways. In fact, it seems to me your income is quite solid, certainly enough to support you and Hannah. Why are you so focused on opening a store?"

Now was neither the time nor the place to get into the emotional battering and sense of vulnerability she carried from her first marriage. Nor did she want to be a *burden* on anyone. That's the term the bishop of her last church had used when she'd said she didn't want to marry Simeon. Freed from the shackles of marriage before Hannah was even born, she was obsessed with never becoming a "burden" ever again.

That is why her own business seemed vital.

"I won't go into details," she summarized in reply to Thomas's question. "But I'll admit I'm ambitious. I've had to be, as a single mother."

"Remember, just because you *work* at a store doesn't mean you're qualified to run your own." He softened the stinging words with a small smile. "But you're smart and determined." Thomas pushed the book across the table toward her. "Abe Yoder said you can keep this as long as you need it. Pull together everything the book recommends and then give it your best shot when you talk to the loan officer."

"I will." She took the book and absently flipped the pages. "And, Thomas, you'll see. I'll prove you wrong."

"I hope so, Emma. I sincerely hope so." He rose. "Well, I'd best be going. Will you be at the house-raising tomorrow?"

"*Ja.* Most of the women will be since we're bringing the food."

"Then I'll see you there." He looked to Hannah. "Can I get a hug goodbye, little one?"

"*Ja.*" The child ran across the room and flung herself into Thomas's arms. He gave her a squeeze and a smacking kiss on her cheek. Then he plopped his straw hat back on his head, nodded and walked out the door.

Through the window, she watched as he kicked off on the bicycle and departed toward the setting sun with a small cloud of dust chasing him.

It annoyed her that he doubted her business acumen. She was determined to show him she was made of tougher stuff. She'd never allow herself to be dependent again.

She *would* prove him wrong. She would.

Chapter Eight

"What else?"

"Some cookies?" suggested Hannah.

"*Ja*, sure, cookies then." Emma packed a batch of cookies in the large hamper she was assembling, nestling the treats among the cold fried chicken and hot hash-brown casserole tucked inside an insulated carrier. "Should we bring some strawberries too?"

"*Ja, ja!*"

"Let's go pick some now, then. That way, they'll be as fresh as possible."

Hannah ran ahead toward the garden while Emma followed with two bowls. The ever-bearing strawberries were on their last run of the summer, and this was an excuse to pick the remainders. She had plenty of the fruit already made into preserves and could spare the rest.

With the child's help, Emma's hamper was soon stuffed with food and ready to bring to the Schrocks' house-raising party. She knew Thomas would be there, and she had mixed emotions about seeing him after last night's devastating analysis of her business hopes.

"*Komm, liebling*, let's get you and the hamper into the wagon. We don't want to be late." Emma shepherded her child outside. Hannah climbed in and took her usual seat on a cushion while Emma placed the hamper behind the child. Then she seized the handle and said, "Remember, tell me everything you see as we go, and I'll do the same."

It was a game she often played with her child while walking. They identified every flower, tree, bush, bird, or other flora and fauna as they saw them. It was a way to keep Hannah occupied, as well as teach the youngster about her surroundings. Deer were common sightings, elk were an occasional treat, bald eagles surprisingly numerous and once they had glimpsed a coyote trotting across the road.

The Schrocks' home site was about a mile away. Emma joined a flow of foot traffic on the way, as well as numerous horse-drawn wagons carrying tools, lumber and other building necessities. It always made her heart swell with satisfaction to be among a group of people with a solid goal in mind. Today's goal was to get a family out of camping in a barn and under a proper roof.

Adam Chupp, who owned a log cabin construction company, was the foreman of the project. Emma pulled the wagon up to where the women were setting up tables and laying out platters and baskets of food under a cluster of stately ponderosa pines. Chatting with some of the women, Emma lifted Hannah from the wagon.

She gave the child strict instructions. "You stay over on this side of the yard, *liebling*," she ordered. "Do you see the concrete basement already in place? Don't go anywhere near it. I don't want you falling in. You can play with the other children, but stay away from the worksite, *ja*?"

"*Ja, Mamm.*" Hannah spied another girl her age and darted away. Emma hoped her daughter would obey. The child had been to many work parties and knew the routine.

Standing for a moment watching Hannah with a fond smile on her face, Emma suddenly spotted Thomas arriving in a buggy with Matthew Miller. He was dressed for construction work, with a tool belt hanging over one shoulder. She was surprised by the flare of butterflies in her midsection, followed instantly by annoyance at both him and herself. She turned aside lest her expression give her away.

For a moment, she stood alone in the midst of the bustling women, reflecting. After her husband had died when she was pregnant with Hannah, she had set herself up for a life of independence, starting with migrating out here to Montana at the suggestion of her aunt and uncle. She had worked hard and set up income streams to support herself and her daughter. Until this point, she had been very pleased with the direction her life was going.

But was it enough? She watched as a woman named Eva Hostetler put her tiny daughter down on the grass. The baby was just learning the skill of walking, and Eva absently guided the youngster's faltering steps while speaking to a friend.

Was it enough for Emma to have just one child? Like most Amish girls, she had dreamed of having a large family when she grew up. Her deceased husband had put an end to that dream in many ways—not just from his behavior and attitude, but because she knew she didn't want any more children with a man like that.

She loved children, and watching Eva steady her baby daughter, Emma suddenly knew she would dearly love to have more little ones of her own one day.

This was something of a seismic shift in her thinking. A year ago—even a month ago—she would have confidently said she never wanted to risk marriage again. Once bitten and twice shy.

But now... Her eyes flicked to Thomas, who was standing attentively among the group of men gathered around the foreman, listening to directions for framing up the house. Maybe things had changed.

Emma sighed and did the only thing she could do—she put the matter into *Gott*'s hands.

Chatting with some of the other women, she unpacked her hamper and spread the food out for when the hungry men would break for lunch. She saw quilting frames being set up to occupy the women during the afternoon when there wouldn't be much for them to do.

The men broke up and scattered to various tasks. Soon the sound of hammering and sawing cut through the air, and Emma smelled the sweet scent of pine lumber.

She saw Sarah Schrock, heavily pregnant, pause to watch the activity, a smile playing on her face. Emma walked over. "Exciting to watch your home being built, *ja*?"

"Ja." The pretty matron's smile broadened. "I won't say it hasn't been exciting camping in the Millers' barn, but it gets old." She patted her belly. "Especially now."

"I can imagine. It's a *gut* turnout today. Between today and tomorrow, you might even be in a position to move in next week while the house is being finished around you."

"Ja, that's what my *hutband* said. I'm thrilled with the idea. And I'm sure the Millers will be happy to have the majority of their barn back too. Eli Miller has been weaving his way amid our boxes and furniture and woodstove all packed into the barn." She paused. "The new man, Thomas Kemp, said he's willing to help us move. He's a *gut* man."

Thomas again. If she didn't know better, Emma would hazard a guess that Sarah was in on the conspiracy to push her toward Thomas. Why else would Sarah specifically mention him? She gave Sarah a suspicious side-eye, but the woman's expression was bland, absolutely innocent of any nefarious intent.

Thomas, Thomas, Thomas. It seemed everything—and everyone—was nudging her toward Thomas. Or maybe it was *Gott*?

She watched him out of the corner of her eye over the course of the morning. The man knew carpentry, no question. He was an active and competent member of the crew, hammering and sawing and measuring with confidence. She was pleased to see a level of camaraderie develop with him among the other men.

"He seems to be doing well," murmured a voice in her ear.

Startled, Emma turned to see her Aunt Lois. "Who?" she asked innocently.

"Thomas. I wondered how much carpentry experience he had, but he seems to be holding his own."

"*Ja*, seems that way." Emma kept her voice bland. "He said he helped his brother and sister-in-law build a house in Indiana before he moved out here, and presumably, he wouldn't have done that if he wasn't already an experienced carpenter."

"He seems like a *gut* man."

Emma's eyes narrowed and a thread of annoyance ran through her. Unquestionably, Aunt Lois was herding her toward the man. It didn't matter that he was in her thoughts more and more lately, she wasn't about to be pushed into anything, as she had been corralled into marrying her late husband. If she ever married again, it would be on her terms, and her terms only.

She decided to take the bull by the horns. "I agree he's a *gut* man, but why do you keep pointing that out to me?"

"Do I?" Aunt Lois had a guileless expression on her

face. She shrugged. "No reason. It's just nice to see some-one new to the community doing so well."

"I see." Emma turned to fiddle with a vase of wild-flowers set on a picnic table. "Aunty, please don't do this. I'm happy being a single mother. I don't want to get re-married."

"I would never push you toward getting remarried, Emma. You should know better than that."

"Maybe not, but sometimes it sure seems that way."

"But don't you think Hannah needs a father?"

"That's not a good enough reason to get married." Emma plucked a dried leaf from the floral arrangement. "You know what my first marriage was like. I'm not going through that again."

"Thankfully, there aren't many men like your first husband, *liebling*. And I greatly doubt Thomas has the faults Simeon had."

"It doesn't matter." Emma softened her words by kiss-ing her aunt on the cheek. "This isn't anything that can be pushed, Aunt Lois."

The older woman sighed. "As you say. *Komm*, we're working on a new quilt for Sarah Schrock's home."

Glancing over to make sure Hannah was all right, Emma walked across to join some of the quilters stitch-ing a beautiful double-wedding-ring pattern.

No, she wouldn't be pushed. And that was that.

If there was one area Thomas felt confident about his skills, it was carpentry. Like most Amish boys, he had learned the trade at his father's knee. Like riding a bi-cycle, he was a little rusty, but he hadn't forgotten. Even during his rebellious years, carpentry had been useful. Once a hammer was back in his hand, the muscle mem-ory returned.

The moment he arrived in Matthew Miller's wagon, he'd spotted Emma. Her trim figure was attired in a dark green dress with a black apron. Her beautiful face was animated as she spoke with another young mother He felt another moment of longing, piercing and unexpected, similar to that emotion he'd felt the evening before. If he wasn't very careful, he could easily become obsessed with Emma Fisher and her daughter.

The home site for the Schrock family already had a concrete basement poured and dried. It was ready to have a home framed up over it. Thomas hooked on his tool belt and stood in a semicircle with the other men as he listened to Adam Chupp's instructions and learned what his particular assignment would be.

"The concrete was poured two weeks ago," Adam was saying, "so we're ready to frame. Two stories." He spread out a blueprint on a card table and stabbed the sheets with a grimy index finger. "Two bathrooms, one upstairs and one downstairs. Kitchen over here, living room there, storage room in this corner. Six bedrooms upstairs. Just between you and me, I think they're expecting more kids." He winked, and a ripple of laughter spread among the men. Thomas joined in. Large families were certainly the norm among church families, so big homes were common. Since homes also doubled as locations to hold church services, the Schrock family no doubt assumed they would slip into the rotation once the house was complete.

"Today," Adam continued, "I want to get the rough framing up. Sidewalls, floor joists, floor insulation. Daniel and Amos will concentrate on plumbing, the rest of us will handle the carpentry. With *Gott*'s help, we'll get the framing done today and can work on the roof tomorrow.

After that, siding. We might be able to get the Schrocks in by late next week. Any questions?"

Thomas stayed silent as various men peppered the foreman with questions and clarifications. Adam answered them all, then he went down the line and assigned everyone specific tasks. Thomas found himself on the crew making up the wall frame for one side. He was partnered with a man named Benjamin Troyer. Thomas saw Benjamin's gaze flick to the scar on his cheek as they filled their tool belt pouches with nails and screws. The scar was a silent reminder of Thomas's need for redemption, his desire to leave his past behind.

Benjamin was a cheerful and fast-working fellow who liked to talk, and who was far too polite to reference Thomas's facial disfigurement.

"And that's how we met," said Benjamin, banging on a nail and concluding the story of how he'd met his wife. "My wife is a veterinarian, of all things. She left the church during her years of schooling then came back when her *mamm* needed some surgery. Our first *bopplin* is due in a few months, and I can't wait to become a father at last. I'd almost given up hope of ever getting married, much less having *kinner*." He chuckled and looked very pleased with himself.

"I'm in that state myself," admitted Thomas. His eyes flickered toward Emma's figure as she set up more tables with the other women. "But there's no one on the horizon for me."

"Trust in *Gott*," Benjamin replied. He snapped out his tape measure, marked a two-by-four and prepared to saw the lumber to the needed length. "He can certainly send the right woman when you least expect it."

"That's what I'd like to think, and you're right. I'll

trust in *Gott.*" *And I'll pray that my past won't ever come back to haunt me*, he added silently.

"So you're from Indiana, you said?"

"Ja." Thomas toenailed two boards together. "My brother and sister live in a town called Chaffinch. My brother just bought a dry goods store out there. He married the woman who was managing it. My sister, Miriam, is still unmarried. She left the church and became a nurse, but something tells me she might come back. I think the *Englisch* world is not quite what she expected."

"Ja, that would be *gut* if she came back. Lots of security by returning to the church." Benjamin banged a nail with vigor. "I think this wall frame is ready to connect to the next one, don't you think?"

The morning progressed. Thomas worked up a decent sweat as the day warmed, but it was more than the work and the temperature. He was warmed by the camaraderie of working with a group of men toward a common goal. The men joked and laughed, sang snatches of songs, and enjoyed themselves.

Frequently, Thomas glanced toward Emma, trying to stay as inconspicuous as possible. He didn't want to show off his skills, exactly—that would be *hochmut*—but he kept his work clean and precise. He had a feeling she was also glancing at him, and he found himself very much wanting to demonstrate he was a good Amish man with normal skills, not the recalcitrant youth he used to be.

After several hours of work, the wall frames were up for the downstairs, with floor joists spanning the basement and insulation fastened between the joists. Some members of the crew were putting plywood flooring across the joists. It was starting to look like a house.

At noon, Adam stood at the edge of the site and gave

a piercing whistle that cut across all the chatter of voices and clatter of tools. "Let's eat!" he shouted.

Thomas realized he was hungry. Hard work truly did create a big appetite. The men unhooked their tool belts and laid them on the ground where they had stopped. Thomas fished a handkerchief from his pocket, mopped his face and then followed the men toward the tables. The women had set things up as a potluck, so he got in line behind Benjamin and soon had a plate.

As each man sat down, he removed his hat, bowed his head and said a silent grace before tucking in to the food. Thomas seated himself next to Adam, the project foreman, paused to offer gratitude to *Gott* for letting him join this new community and prayed for guidance to continue conducting himself in a worthy manner.

"So you have a log home business, *ja*?" he asked Adam.

"That's right." Adam bit into a biscuit and spoke with his mouth full. "And it's booming. I have as much business as I can handle. I'm looking to hire someone. Are you interested?"

Thomas chuckled. "I'm working full time at the Yoder's, so I wouldn't have time. Do you need an experienced carpenter?"

"Not especially. I'm willing to train. I thought about asking at the local high school to see if there's a kid who wants a job…"

Suddenly, a little body pushed in between Thomas and Adam. "Hi! Hi!" cried Hannah.

He turned to the child. "*Guder mariye*, little one. Should you be here? Where's your *mamm*?"

"There." The toddler pointed, and Thomas glanced over to see Emma in a similar stance as she'd had after the Sabbath service—scanning the crowd to find her daughter, an annoyed expression on her face.

He raised his arm and waved, caught her eye, and pointed toward Hannah standing next to him. Emma's face cleared and she marched over to the table.

"*Liebling*, I told you not to bother the men," she scolded.

"She's not bothering me, but it looked like you lost track of her for a bit."

"*Ja.*" Emma swung the child onto her hip and then lingered a moment. "The building is going well."

"Seems to be. Adam here is a *gut* foreman. He's all go. It's hard to keep up."

Adam chuckled. "It feels *gut* to work hard."

"*Ja.* Well, I'll do better to keep Hannah out of the way." Emma turned and Thomas could hear her quietly scold the child. It was a shame, really. He wished he could think of an excuse to keep them both closer.

"She seems to like you," observed Adam, taking a bite of chicken.

For a panicked moment, Thomas thought the other man referred to Emma. To counter that possibility, he deflected attention to the child. "She's a cute little toddler, ain't so? It's been a while since I've been around young *kinner*, and I miss them."

"*Ja*, that's why I'm looking forward to having one of my own."

Thomas breathed a sigh of relief. The other man apparently *had* been referring to Hannah, not Emma. He hoped his interest in the young widow was not branded on his forehead.

He kept the conversation generic through lunch. After the meal, he deposited his dishes in a large tub and returned to work. As he continued to help frame up the house, he watched as the women cleared dishes, packed away food, and settled down to sedentary activities such as sewing or quilting.

Adam set some of the older boys to simpler carpentry tasks. Babies and toddlers—including Hannah—were bedded down on quilts or makeshift cradles for naps. The other children continued to play games, chasing each other among the trees and shrieking with laughter.

For a moment, Thomas paused to savor the scene. It was similar to so many construction sites he had been to as a child and a teen, until his rebellion and anger had chased him away. As a *youngie*, he had taken it for granted and hadn't appreciated what he'd had. But he realized now the importance of how he'd grown up—the continuity, the community, the faith, the camaraderie. How could he ever give that up again?

He hoped for a hundred more house- or barn-raisings. He wanted to be part of them all. He had missed too much during his rebellious years. He had a lot to make up for.

And maybe—he could only hope—*Gott* had a plan for him. He glanced at Emma sitting demurely before a quilting frame.

For an electrifying moment, he caught Emma's eye. The moment lengthened then he quickly turned his attention once more to the carpentry job at hand. He swallowed hard and tried not to read too much into that enigmatic look.

He hadn't met the eyes of any other woman throughout the day. Just Emma's. It meant she was watching him covertly, just as he was watching her. He hoped it meant what he hoped it meant.

But Emma was the bishop's niece. He was a former jailbird. What chance could he possibly have with her?

Chapter Nine

On Sunday morning, Thomas stood at his window in the boardinghouse and looked down at the quiet street. It was an off-Sunday, so there was no church service and, frankly, he wondered what he was going to do with himself all day.

At times like these, his lack of family became an acute longing. How well he remembered slow Sundays in Indiana—people walking to others' houses for visits, lemonade sipped on shady front porches, children playing in yards. As an older teen, he'd felt contempt for such wholesome activities and a longing to stir up trouble, a desire for action, notice, attention.

He gave a small snort at his own youthful folly. What a difference a year made. Now, the last thing he desired was a spotlight. He wanted to sink into anonymity, to make no waves or ripples, to attract no attention. He simply wanted to prove himself a worthy man.

He knew how close he'd gotten to making an irredeemable mess of his life. He closed his eyes and whispered a prayer of gratitude to *Gott*. It was *Gott* who had swayed Joseph to pay for the attorney, who'd ultimately been able to clear him of that devastating charge of involuntary manslaughter. He might otherwise still be sitting in jail today.

Instead… He opened his eyes and peered at the sidewalks below to where a dressed-up family was heading toward a church building. Instead, he was here, in this little town, working with a community of nice people…none of whom knew about his past. Except the bishop, of course.

A figure walking down the sidewalk caught his idle gaze. Thomas's eyes narrowed. It was the same teen he'd seen in the store the week before. The one who'd snatched the bag of candy. There was something about the boy's posture that Thomas recognized. He, too, had walked in the same way—hunched, furtive—when he'd been up to mischief.

On impulse, Thomas turned, snatched up his hat and left his room. Matthew Miller wasn't at the front desk and no one else saw him leave the boardinghouse.

He glimpsed the teen easily ahead of him. He was wearing a distinctive blue T-shirt and had greasy brown hair. Thomas hurried to catch up until he was a discreet distance behind.

The boy was heading for the small city park. It was a popular place for young families since it boasted many large and beautiful shade trees, an abundance of picnic tables and a large playground. This early on a Sunday morning, it was deserted, though it bore evidence of activities from the day before. There were a few items of litter scattered around, and the garbage cans overflowed with paper plates and other picnic debris.

Thomas watched as the boy went up to one of the garbage cans next to a large maple tree. He reached in and, in a few moments, Thomas saw a wisp of smoke. The teen smirked with evident satisfaction and moved on to the next garbage can.

Thomas slipped up behind the youth and seized his wrist, wrenching the lighter out of the boy's hand. "Bad decision," he remarked.

Caught by surprise, the teen dropped some offensive language and turned to clout Thomas, who ducked with the ease of long experience.

"Let me go!" the boy cried.

"Not until we make sure the fire is out in that other garbage can. Come along."

To Thomas's surprise, the teen allowed himself to be yanked by the shirt toward the smoking receptacle. The fire had not caught. Thomas reached in, snatched out the smoldering paper plates and dropped them to the ground. "Stomp on them," he ordered the boy.

Shrugging, the youth stomped on the trash until the smoldering stopped. Then he stood there sulking, his brown eyes narrowed.

"What's your name, kid?" Thomas stepped back and crossed his hands on his chest.

"Jeremy," replied the youth, staring at the charred paper plates.

"And where are your parents?"

An ugly expression crossed the boy's face. "They don't care about me," he snarled.

"So you thought shoplifting from Yoder's Mercantile and setting fire to garbage cans would help?"

An expression of wary surprise crossed the boy's face. "How did you know I took something from that store?"

"Because I work there and I saw you."

"But you didn't stop me."

Thomas smiled thinly. "My coworkers tried to stop you, and you gave them the slip. Believe it or not, kid, I was in your shoes a few years ago. I got very good at shoplifting. I never set fire to garbage cans, but I did a lot of worse stuff. That's behind me now."

"Hooray for you," the boy replied sarcastically.

"Don't you want to know *why* it's behind me?"

"No."

Thomas overrode the objection. "It's because a year ago I got framed for a horrific crime I didn't commit back in Indiana. Ever have someone accuse you of involuntary manslaughter?" He tapped his cheek. "Ever have your face slashed by a gang leader? Ever sit in jail wondering if that was going to be your new home? Well, that was me last year."

"What happened?" Jeremy looked reluctant interested. His gaze flicked to Thomas's facial scar.

"My brother was able to hire a lawyer to present some critical evidence, and the thug who actually caused someone to die was caught and prosecuted. That's what happens when you run with the wrong crowd. I learned that the hard way."

The youth eyed Thomas's straw hat. "But aren't you part of that new church outside town?"

"*Ja*, I am. And that, my boy, is what saved me."

"Yeah, right." Jeremy stepped back and shoved his hands into his pockets.

"No more setting fires, okay?" Thomas gave the teen a look of sympathy. "It can only end badly."

The youth didn't say anything for a moment, then he suddenly blurted, "You guys build houses, don't you?"

Surprised by the unexpected question, Thomas replied, "*Ja*. That is, we build houses for each other. More people from our church community are moving here, and they need places to live." He paused. "Why?"

"Nothing."

"Are you interested in carpentry?"

"Maybe." The boy averted his eyes in a skittish manner and looked across the park. "Gotta go." He loped off.

Thomas pocketed the lighter and watched the teen hurry away. His heart ached with sympathy for the youth. It sounded like his home life was not the best. Instinct told Thomas the kid was crying out for attention, for guidance, for help.

He also knew that without intervention, the boy was likely to escalate his bad behavior until something irreversible happened. "Been there, done that," he muttered.

But he was clueless as to what could be done to intervene. All he knew was the kid's first name. Besides, he was new in town himself, and he had no idea of the town's dynamics or how it handled recalcitrant youth. He didn't know if this isolated rural community had problems with domestic violence or gang activity or any other social ill.

Yet he still felt intense sympathy for Jeremy. During all his own wild adolescence, at least he'd had good parents—until his escapades had caused his father to distractedly get into the horrible buggy accident that had killed them.

Thomas sighed. "Forgive me, *Gott*," he whispered.

He still wondered if he was worthy of forgiveness.

But if there was one thing he'd learned on his hard and rocky journey, it was how even the most irredeemable people could be redeemed. Even himself.

Perhaps even Jeremy.

In a thoughtful frame of mind, he walked back across the park toward the boardinghouse. The deep shade from the park's stately maples punctuated the sunny grassy areas. Eyes on the ground, Thomas slowly realized he was walking over many winged maple seeds scattered beneath the parent trees. He stopped, stared for a moment, and then bent and picked one up.

He twirled the seed back and forth in his hand. The Bible was full of verses referencing seeds—their potential, the need for proper sowing, the benefits of a fruitful harvest. In all mentions, man could plant and water, but only *Gott* could cause the seed to grow.

Had he just planted a seed today with the teen? he wondered. He dropped the maple seed and watched it spiral to the ground.

Walking back to the boardinghouse, his thoughts drifted to Emma. She and Hannah had been at the house-building event both Friday and yesterday, but after Hannah's small naughtiness on Friday, Emma had kept the child away from him. He was reluctant to speak to Emma—a reluctance, he knew, that stemmed from his own feelings of unworthiness, compounded by the fiscal reality he had explained when he'd helped her with her business plan.

He hesitated to push in where he wasn't wanted, either personally or professionally. Yet was he building barriers in his mind where none existed?

Returning to the courtyard of the boardinghouse, he saw the bicycle Abe Yoder had loaned him standing near a wall on its kickstand. It was an off-Sunday. Emma was likely to be home and at leisure. If he were to ride over to see her, it would not be outside the bounds of propriety. Just paying a friendly Sunday visit…

Yet he knew such a visit could easily be construed as courting behavior.

Suddenly, Thomas didn't care. He could plant a seed of interest, Emma could water it, but only *Gott* could bring a courtship to fruition. Before he could expect others to forgive him, maybe he had to forgive himself first. His past was in his past. Maybe it was time to look toward the future.

Thomas pulled the bicycle up, pushed away the kickstand and took off down the quiet streets of town toward the Amish settlement. The warm air blew on his face and he clamped his straw hat down more firmly. Emma might be off visiting others, in which case this trip would be a waste of time. But maybe she would be home. He would leave the matter up to *Gott*.

Emma was fighting a losing battle with the Sabbath edict to rest versus her desire to work in the garden. Weeding and cultivating her beloved plants wasn't "work" to her, or so she told herself. She longed to wade out among the verdant growing area and busy herself weeding, but it would set a poor example to her daughter.

Instead, she sat in one of the two rocking chairs on the shaded porch facing the garden, Hannah in her lap, and read the child stories from a children's Bible.

Pointing to an illustration of animals being loaded onto Noah's ark, Emma paused the story and asked her daughter, "How many animals can you identify?"

"Zebra." Hannah pointed.

"*Gut!* What else?"

"Giraffe."

"*Ja.*"

"Lion."

"Smart girl! *Ja...*"

The child was sleepy and not inclined to concentrate, so Emma didn't tax her further. Instead, she continued to read the narrative.

A crunching sound interrupted her concentration. She looked over and saw Thomas pedaling on the road, his bicycle tires scrunching the gravel.

She refused to admit she was pleased to see him. Instead, she tried to recapture the annoyance she'd felt over the matter of the business plan.

Her daughter had no such compunction. Instantly, the child's sleepiness departed and she jerked upright in Emma's lap. "Mr. Thomas! Mr. Thomas!"

Thomas coasted to a stop, dismounted and wheeled the bike into the yard. Hannah wiggled off Emma's lap, clambered down the porch steps and ran toward the man. "Hi! Hi!"

"*Guder mariye*, little one." Thomas pushed down the kickstand on the bike and lifted Hannah into his arms. He walked toward the porch.

Emma smoothed her apron. "I'm surprised to see you."

"I was bored," he admitted. "It's quiet in town, so I came to see if I'm forgiven for pushing you too hard on the business proposal."

She shrugged. "I'll admit I wasn't too happy, but then I read through that book you left and realized I have to take the matter a little more seriously than I was. I've been working on it."

"When is your appointment with the banker?"

"Tomorrow."

"Do you want me to look over the proposal?"

"It's Sunday. We're not supposed to be doing any work, remember?"

"*Ja*, I know. Okay, then would you like to hear an interesting encounter I had a little while ago?"

"*Ja*, sure." She rose. "I have lemonade in the icebox. Would you like a glass?"

"*Danke*." Thomas mounted the porch steps, put Hannah down and then seated himself in the other porch rocker.

Emma entered her cabin and pulled a jar of lemonade

from the icebox. She poured three glasses—a small one for Hannah—and placed a few cookies on a plate. She loaded everything onto a tray all while wondering why Thomas had come.

The trouble with Sunday visits between two single people was they could easily be interpreted as a courting move. She knew Thomas knew this. Was his presence here a deliberate move with that in mind?

But she could hardly tell him to go away. She didn't *want* to tell him to go away.

She went back out on the porch and placed the tray on the table between the rocking chairs. Hannah had climbed onto Thomas's lap and was showing him the book she had been reading, chattering about the animals going into Noah's ark.

Emma sank down in her rocker. "So you were bored, eh?"

"*Ja.* No work today, no church today and I didn't have anything to do." He reached for a glass.

"And what was this interesting encounter you mentioned?"

Thomas leaned back in the rocker and Hannah snuggled herself against his chest, just as she might do if he were her father. Emma swallowed and tried not to dwell on the child's obsession.

"I managed to stop a teenage boy from setting fire to some garbage cans in the town park," he began.

Emma jerked her head up. "You're kidding!"

"No. It was the same kid who snatched a bag of candy from the Yoder's store that one time you tried to stop him. I learned his name is Jeremy. Here's what happened…" Thomas related the entire incident.

Emma felt the familiar revulsion toward the youth. "He's trouble, that boy."

"*Ja*, he is. But he also reminds me of...of someone I used to know back in Indiana."

"The kid should be in jail."

Thomas looked at her with surprise. "It's not like you to be so hostile," he observed. "I agree the kid needs help, but why do his antics bother you so much?"

"He's a juvenile delinquent. People like him cause nothing but problems." She couldn't keep the bitterness out of her voice. "I should know. I married one."

She wanted to snatch the words back, but it was too late.

Thomas looked at her with something akin to compassion. "So *that* accounts for your attitude."

"I won't deny it." She gave a frustrated sigh, and glanced at her daughter. The child's sleepiness had caught up with her and she dozed against Thomas's shirt. "And you know the ironic thing? By sheer coincidence, the kid physically resembles my husband when he was younger. It's unreasonable of me to react so strongly, but there you go."

"You can't take out your earlier insecurities on some random kid," he told her.

"Thank you for that bit of psychological analysis," she snapped, then slapped a hand over her mouth. "I'm sorry, you're right. And now I'm taking it out on you." Emma realized her visceral reaction to the teen was irrational, but even the thought of the boy set her teeth on edge.

"I find myself wanting to help him," Thomas remarked.

"Why?" She took a calming breath. "Okay, that sounded uncharitable. But can someone like that be helped?"

"Possibly. I think the best thing to do is distract him from his misdeeds. He mentioned an interest in carpentry. At the house-raising, Adam Chupp mentioned he's looking to hire someone. I wonder if I could connect Adam to this kid? Maybe Adam could offer him a job."

Emma was startled. "But I assume Jeremy isn't experienced. Wouldn't Adam need someone who knows his way around tools?"

"Maybe yes, maybe no. I don't know. Adam did say he might contact the local high school to find someone. At any rate, it seems the boy needs some structure and training to get him straightened out." Thomas rubbed his chin. "Of course, I don't know his last name or how to get hold of him again, so maybe this thought is just blowing sunshine."

"Well, you're a better person than I am," she admitted.

Thomas looked at her and then down at the brown hair and small white *kapp* of the child in his arms. "That's a new development," he muttered.

Emma raised her eyebrows. What was it about this man's past that haunted him? She decided to simply ask. "Why do you always underrate yourself, Thomas? What happened to you before you came here to Montana that makes you doubt yourself?"

It was as if a literal shutter had dropped over his face. His expression blanked into neutrality. "Nothing."

She managed a small snort of disbelief. "That's the most transparent lie I've heard in a long time. It's obvious you're politely telling me to mind my own business."

"*Ja*, I guess I am." He tempered the words with a small smile of his own.

"What brought you to Montana?"

He shrugged a bit defensively. "Opportunity, what else? I've always been something of a rolling stone, restless, curious to see new places. I heard about this settlement, and Montana was a place I'd never been to. I wrote to your uncle and told him what my qualifications were as far as bookkeeping and even computer skills, and I asked if there were any jobs available. He knew the Yoders were looking for a bookkeeper. The rest is history."

The truth and nothing but the truth, but not the whole truth, Emma thought. She instinctively knew he was leaving out huge chunks of what had motivated him to leave his home behind and move fifteen hundred miles away.

But it was too early into their acquaintance to press. Instead, she asked, "And you said you want to be baptized? Why weren't you baptized earlier?"

"Because I left the church and lived in the *Englisch* world for a long time." He gazed out at the verdant garden, his eyes a bit unfocused as if he were looking inward. "I learned a lot—my computer skills, for instance—but it was a harsh place. I finally came to my senses and realized I have a lot more to gain within the church community than outside of it. So here I am."

"What do you think of Montana so far?"

His eyes locked with hers. "It's everything I could hope for."

Oh, yes, he was interested in courting. Emma could not deny it any more than she could deny Hannah's uncanny fondness for this man. But how did she feel about him? Aside from her reluctance to abandon her rebellious interest in staying single, there was something of a mystery about Thomas. She wasn't about to let herself get overly fond of him—or worse, let her daughter become overly fond of him—without a thorough understanding of his character and motivation. And that included the elusive past he kept avoiding.

Nervously, she dropped her gaze and fiddled with the strings of her *kapp*. Anxious to change the subject, she asked, "Would you be interested in looking over what I've done with the business proposal after all?"

"Even though it's a Sunday? *Ja*, sure."

He started to rise with the sleeping child in his arms, but she forestalled him. "*Nein*, stay there. I'll get it." She slipped into the house and snatched up the neatly written paperwork she had copied and recopied. It looked quite professional, if she did say so herself.

She emerged back onto the porch and placed the proposal on the small table next to him. "Here, I'll take Hannah."

He transferred the child into her arms, picked up the paperwork and began reading. She watched his face for clues of what he thought of it, but he gave no indication. Instead, he read silently, turned pages, read some more.

After ten minutes, he laid the documents down on the table. "You've made the best of what you have," he said. "Clearly, you've taken the lessons from that book to heart. Now it's up to the bank's loan officer."

"Do you think he'll approve?"

"*Nein*," he said gently. "I don't. I could be wrong, but you need to prepare yourself for that possibility."

She tried to shrug off the sense of bleakness that enveloped her at her dream being dashed. Thomas thought she was pinning too much hope on what he saw as an unlikely event.

But if the loan fell through, she didn't know what else she was going to do to achieve the financial security she craved.

She didn't want to give up her dreams of financial freedom and the stability she was determined to obtain. Thomas, no matter how attractive, was not the answer to those problems.

Chapter Ten

On Monday morning, Emma tucked the thin notebook with her business proposal into a satchel along with a few sample bars of soap. Before she left for town, she took her daughter over to her aunt and uncle's so Aunt Lois could watch Hannah during the day. "Remember, if you're a *gut* girl for Aunt Lois, I'll take you to the playground tomorrow," she bribed the child.

"Your appointment with the banker isn't until later afternoon, *ja*?" asked Aunt Lois. "I'll say a prayer it goes well."

"Danke." Emma kissed her daughter and walked to town for a day of work at the store.

"What time is your appointment?" asked Mabel Yoder when Emma arrived for work. Her boss knew about the meeting.

"Four o'clock. I'll be able to put in nearly a full day's work," Emma replied. "Is there a safe place to put my satchel? It has the business plan in it, and I don't want it to get messed up."

"Leave it with Thomas."

Once again, Emma got the impression her boss was colluding to push her toward Thomas, but there was no denying his office was unlikely to have any disturbances for her precious paperwork.

She approached the back room and saw Thomas bent over a ledger. She gave a quick knock on the doorframe. *"Guder mariye."*

He lifted his head and smiled. *"Guder mariye."*

"Mabel suggested your office might be the best place to put my satchel for safekeeping until my appointment this afternoon."

"Ja, sure." He rose and reached for the notebook. "Nervous?"

"Ja, a bit." She lingered a moment. "And I know it's belated, but *danke* for working with me on the business plan."

He shrugged. "Glad to help."

She nodded her thanks and left to work in the main part of the store.

The day seemed to crawl and Emma found herself clock-watching like she had never done before. At last it was time to leave. She slipped into the washroom to make sure her *kapp* was neat and no stray hairs had escaped. She straightened her apron, took a deep breath and went to fetch the satchel from Thomas's office.

"I'll say a prayer," he offered.

"Danke." She said her goodbyes to Mabel Yoder and stepped outside the door into the late-afternoon sunshine.

The bank was only two blocks away. Emma paused before the dark glass doors, glanced at the satchel in her hands and entered the building.

"I'm here to see Jack Thompson," she told one of the tellers.

"His office is right over there." The young woman pointed.

Emma nodded and walked toward an office. "Mr. Thompson?"

A middle-aged man with a short beard was working on a computer. He rose from his desk chair. "You must be Ms. Fisher."

"*Ja.* How do you do?" She shook his hand with a confidence she did not feel and took the seat he indicated.

He sat back behind his desk. "I understand you're interested in a startup business loan for opening a store," he said. "Is that correct?"

"*Ja.* I'd like to rent and renovate that small vacant building right next to Yoder's Mercantile."

"I'm familiar with it." The man smiled. "I must say, it's been wonderful watching the Amish set up businesses here in Pierce. As a whole, I'm deeply impressed with the industriousness and business savvy of the church members."

"Thank you." Emma brightened and felt more hopeful.

"We've made a couple of loans to church members," continued the banker as he tapped something on the keyboard. "As a group, they are an excellent financial risk."

"I agree." Emma's confidence surged.

"Now, let's discuss your plans," Mr. Thompson continued. "What is it you want to do to the building? I assume you'll need to renovate it to suit your needs. What kind of business do you have in mind?"

"Soap," stated Emma. "Handmade soap." She reached into the satchel and withdrew three sample bars.

"Soap?" Thompson's voice scaled up. He eyed the bars.

"*Ja.* I'm an expert soap maker. My bars are sold at Yoder's, and I have to restock the display almost daily."

"Is that all you plan to sell?" inquired Thompson. He picked up one of the samples. "Just soap?"

"*J-ja,*" she stuttered. "I am confident the market here in Pierce will support the business."

"Pierce has a very small population," stated Thompson. "Less than four thousand people. Where else do you plan to market your product?"

"N-nowhere." Emma was trying hard not to be cowed by the suited man sitting across from her, but it wasn't easy. "I—I have a business plan, if you're interested in seeing it." She proffered the slender notebook.

"Yes, thank you." Thompson replaced the soap on the desk, took the notebook, flipped it open and began to read.

In the sudden silence, Emma heard faint recorded music playing in the background. She glanced around at the neutral pictures on the walls, the polished desk and chairs, the plush carpet. A clock ticked loudly.

At last, Thompson looked up. "I don't want to be too discouraging, Ms. Fisher, but I don't believe we can loan you any money based on what's in this notebook."

All her dreams threatened to shatter like glass. "B-but I can assure you, Mr. Thompson, no one makes better soap than me."

"I have no doubt of your skills, but running a business requires more than just the ability to make a product. It requires rock-solid skills in other aspects. According to this—" he tapped the open notebook with the business plan "—your marketing strategies and sales channels for your proposed business are very weak. Considering that Pierce is so far off the beaten track and cannot anticipate a large tourist market, all your business would depend on foot traffic. To be frank, Ms. Fisher, I don't think the town can support such a specialized business."

"But…but…my soap sells so well at Yoder's!"

"I'm sure it does. But with your own store, do you anticipate selling enough to cover utilities, insurance, rent, and still repay the bank loan? And that doesn't count what you would want to pay yourself as well." He shook his head. "Your financial analysis is not strong enough, Ms. Fisher. I'm sorry to disappoint, but I could never get this loan approved by the lending department."

All her hopes of financial independence came tumbling down. "Is there nothing I can do to convince you I'm a safe bet?" She spoke quietly to battle the tears of frustration welling up.

"About the only thing I can suggest is to find a co-signer," he replied. "And I wouldn't put much hope in that. Your proposal seems too risky."

"You seem determined to shut me down," she said with some asperity.

"I'm just trying to avoid causing you trouble," Thompson replied. He softened his words with a fatherly smile. "Taking out a loan for a business that is highly likely to fail would not just put you in an insurmountable amount of debt, but it would affect your credit rating for future loans. If you're truly determined to start a soap business, you might do better to sell online through a website."

"I see." Selling only through a website was as likely as seeing snow in July. Suddenly, she was desperate to get out of the bank lest Mr. Thompson should see her cry. She stood and reached for the binder. "I'm sorry to have taken up your time, Mr. Thompson."

"And I'm sorry to have to deny your request, Ms. Fisher." He stood and gathered up the sample soap bars for her to pack in her satchel. He sniffed at one of the bars. "These are beautiful," he admitted. "I sincerely hope you can grow your business without the need for a loan, because it's obvious you're very talented."

Somewhat mollified, she gestured toward the bars. "Keep them. I have plenty at home. Good afternoon, Mr. Thompson."

She stumbled out of the bank, blinking in the bright

sunlight, and tried to come to grips with the idea that she would never be able to renovate the building and have her own store. It was not lost on Emma that the banker's concerns echoed Thomas's.

She felt crushed, like her entire goal of financial security had been thrown back in her face. Was *Gott* angry with her?

Unless she could convince someone to cosign a loan with her…? She thought through those she was closest to. Uncle Samuel and Aunt Lois certainly had the highest standing in the church community, but they were not in a position to financially sponsor her. She would never dream of burdening them with such an obligation.

What about the Yoders? She wasn't certain what their financial standing was, but they certainly weren't hurting for money. The success of their mercantile certainly bespoke of sound business sense. Any bank would take a cosigning from Yoder's Mercantile with great seriousness.

Yes, the Yoders were the most likely bet. Mabel and Abe liked her. They trusted her. Surely she could convince them she was a solid risk?

Her vision cleared, she strode toward the mercantile.

Thomas rose from his chair, stretched out his back and shut the ledgers on the desk in front of him. It was just a few minutes before the store closed for the day, and he went toward the cash register, as was his habit, to get the day's tally.

Mabel was busy adding up numbers, and he knew better than to disturb her concentration. Idly, he watched as Abe gently rounded up a few straggling customers, letting them know the store would be closing shortly. Amos Yoder had already closed down the bakery and coffee sections and was busy disinfecting the playthings in the toddler area. All in all, it was a typical end-of-day routine.

He wondered how Emma's appointment had gone.

"Ready," called Mabel.

"Ja, gut," he replied. He joined her behind the cash register and, together, they recorded the day's sales and provided Thomas with the following morning's list of vendor payouts.

The bell over the door jingled and Thomas looked up to see Emma, two bright spots of color in her cheeks. He smiled, but his words of greeting died in his mouth.

She looked shell-shocked, walking like an automaton. She ignored him and zeroed in on Mabel, who was still fussing with the day's receipts.

"How did it go?" he inquired as she approached the cash register.

"Mabel, do you and Abe have a moment?" she asked in a strained voice. "I have a question for you."

Mabel looked at her in surprise. *"Ja,* sure," the older woman answered and raised her voice. "Abe? Emma's here. She has a question…"

Abe lumbered over. *"Guder nammidaag,* Emma. How did your appointment with the banker go?"

Thomas noticed Emma's hands shook as she cleared her throat.

"I have a serious question to ask you both," she said. "Would you consider cosigning a loan for me to secure the loan I need to open a store next door?"

There was a shocked silence. Thomas watched as Abe and Mabel exchanged a lightning glance. The air became heavy with the pregnant pause.

"No," Thomas said into the void. "Abe and Mabel, I do not recommend this."

Emma whirled. "Who asked you?" she hissed in a vicious tone as she glared at him.

"Nobody," he replied, keeping his voice even. "But as the store's bookkeeper, it's my business to safeguard the Yoders' business interests. If you're asking them to cosign a loan, I can only imagine it's because the banker turned you down. That must mean he didn't feel your business plan was strong enough to justify the risk. So, no, I don't recommend the Yoders should cosign a loan for you."

"Emma, dear, you know we'd do anything for you," inserted Abe gently. "But I can't help but feel Thomas is right in this instance."

"Ja," agreed Mabel. "If the bank turned you down, we can't jeopardize our own business by funding something that might fail. We've worked too hard to take a risk like that."

"This is your fault." Emma turned furiously upon Thomas. "You're trying to thwart my plans."

"Emma!" exclaimed Abe.

Her words cut across Thomas like a knife, but he knew he was in the right. "No, I'm trying to prevent everyone from taking too large a risk. You included. You're only looking at a rosy possibility, Emma, not a harsh financial reality. If your idea for a business fails, you—or the Yoders, if they cosigned—could be facing some serious repercussions."

"But what about me?" wailed Emma. "Everything I've worked for is disappearing."

Mabel slipped an arm around Emma's shoulders. "Everything, *liebling*? You've lost nothing except a dream. You're doing fine financially, aren't you? You're so clever at everything you do and make. We'll always be happy to sell everything you provide, as well as employ you as long as we can. Maybe Thomas is right, opening your own store is just too uncertain, especially in a town this size."

Thomas found himself concerned about Emma's level of urgency—almost hysteria—associated with her determination to start this business. He had warned her about the risks. The banker had confirmed those warnings, and now the Yoders agreed. Yet she still lamented the loss.

Why couldn't she see the hazards involved? Why couldn't she understand how unrealistic her proposal was? She was such an intelligent woman, so independent and confident, that this blind spot seemed completely out of character.

There was something wrong here, something deeper than just the thwarting of a business fantasy. He wondered, not for the first time, what lay beneath this sense of urgency.

He watched as Mabel spoke soothing words. He saw the drooping shoulders and the bent head. Emma seemed beaten down, something he'd never expected to see.

If, as he hardly dared hope, there was a possibility of a future with her, he had to get to the bottom of this issue. He needed to find an opportunity to talk to her privately and hoped she would open up about what drove her.

"Emma, would you like me to drive you home?" Abe offered. "It's a long walk for you."

"Nein, danke." Emma slipped away from Mabel's comforting arm and straightened her shoulders in a gesture that was both defiant and crushingly sad. "I need some time to think. The walk will do me good."

Her eyes were bright with unshed tears, but Thomas admired her strength as she appeared to come to grips with the events of the last hour. Without another word, she turned and walked out the door.

The trio was silent a moment and then Mabel sighed. "I hope she'll be okay."

"It will take her some time to get over it," agreed Abe. He clapped Thomas on the back. "*Danke*, my boy, for stepping in and defending us against the idea of cosigning. We love Emma, but that's something we couldn't do."

"*Bitte,*" he replied. He ran a hand through his hair. "I was just thinking there's something not right here, something driving her that seems irrational. I know it's a blow to have her dream of her own store get dashed, but it almost seems there's something more."

Abe rubbed his chin. "She does seem driven," he agreed.

Mabel looked at them. "You fools," she said. "She's a single mother. Enough said."

"But she seems to be doing so well!" Thomas exclaimed.

"You have no idea what kind of insecurity a woman experiences when she's raising a child on her own," retorted Mabel. "My sister was widowed young, and she told me becoming the main breadwinner on top of being the only parent leaves a scar that never goes away. I know my sister never lost that drive to earn money—however she could—to support her children."

"But your sister remarried," observed Abe.

"*Ja*, and I suspect part of that decision was financial," replied Mabel. "Her second marriage has been a happy one, but I'll never forget what she went through when she was faced with raising three little ones on her own."

"So you think Emma's drive stems from being widowed?" asked Thomas.

"She's never said anything, of course, but that's my suspicion." Mabel nodded. "Emma is smart and resourceful, so I can think of no other reason she would stubbornly cling to this idea of having her own store."

"I see." Thomas was left thoughtful. Mabel's theory made sense in so many ways.

Emma figured more and more in his mind. He realized he did, indeed, want a future for her. It was one of the underlying reasons he himself strove to establish himself, not just in the community, but with his own business. He wanted a means to support a family.

Emma had made it clear she was in no hurry to remarry…yet she seemed frantic to establish herself financially. Would she welcome the opportunity to join forces and strive for that together? It seemed a harsh and clinical reason to marry.

Of course, that wouldn't be the only reason for him. He was falling in love with Emma as well as her daughter. How could he ever hope to convince her that he was a good risk?

Chapter Eleven

While walking to her aunt and uncle's to retrieve her daughter, Emma took the opportunity to have a good cry, heaving her grief into a handkerchief. She knew it would leave her face blotchy and unattractive—and spark concerned inquiries from her relatives—but it relieved the immediate emotion. By the time she made her way up the walkway and past her aunt's garden, she was feeling more composed.

But her ravaged face betrayed her. Aunt Lois drew up short when Emma walked into the kitchen. "Child! Are you okay?"

"Nein. I just got turned down by the bank." Emma collapsed onto a kitchen chair and looked around. "Where's Hannah?"

"Napping." The older woman also drew out a chair and sat down. Meanwhile, Uncle Samuel emerged from his office and joined them.

"They turned you down?" he inquired.

"Ja." Emma related her interview and even mentioned her attempt to ask the Yoders to cosign.

Uncle Samuel looked shocked and shook his head at

this revelation. "They have no business cosigning a loan for you, *liebling*," he chastised.

"I know that now. I guess I was just desperate, is all. I thought about asking you to cosign, but I know you aren't in the financial place to do so." She sniffed and mopped her eyes with the sodden handkerchief. "So it's back to square one, I guess."

"*Nein*, Emma, it's not," said Aunt Lois firmly. "You're doing very well for yourself already, thanks to your cleverness and skills. A store would have been a new adventure, but it's not your only opportunity to make a living. In fact, it might have proven more difficult. Running a store full time with a toddler would not have been easy."

"I had that all figured out," she began defensively, and then gave an irritated wave of her hand. "But what does it matter now?"

"Emma." Her uncle folded his hands on the table and looked at her gravely. "Have you thought about remarrying? The Good Lord never meant for us to go through life without a helpmate, especially when children are involved. Hannah needs a father too."

"I have no intention of ever remarrying," she blurted. Instantly, she wished she could snatch the words back.

Both her aunt and uncle wore identical expressions of shock at her declaration. Uncle Samuel's mouth had dropped open and he closed it. "Where did this streak of stubbornness come from?"

Emma firmed her jaw. "It's been my deep dark secret. I won't be forced to remarry for financial reasons," she said. "It's why I've worked so hard to be independent."

"There's more to a marriage than just finances," her uncle said gently. "There are matters of the heart as well. It's not in Hannah's best interest to be raised by a single

mother, especially when there's a fine eligible man standing in the wings whose heart you've already captured."

"You mean Thomas." She almost smiled. "But he himself has admitted he's not in a position to support a family yet."

"Yet," Samuel repeated. "The operative word is 'yet.'
He's hardworking and determined, and I know he would
welcome the chance to court you. You could certainly
do worse."

She shook her head. "Uncle Samuel, please don't push.
I'm simply not ready to get married again, and I'm going
to keep working hard to make sure I don't *have* to. I may
never be ready."

"*Never* is a long time," Aunt Lois said. She cocked
her head, listening. "I think someone is just waking up
from her nap."

"I'll get her." Glad to escape the unwelcome line of
questioning, Emma rose to fetch her daughter from the
little trundle bed in her aunt and uncle's bedroom.

She could hear her aunt and uncle murmuring from
the kitchen and knew they were discussing her stance.
She firmed her lips. They both well knew how disastrous
her first marriage had been, and it annoyed her that they
should push her toward a second marriage, especially following her disappointing meeting with the loan officer.

She emerged from the bedroom with the sleepy toddler resting on her shoulder. "I'd best be going," she told
them. "I have chores to do and dinner to cook, and I
promised Hannah I'll take her to the park tomorrow so
she can play on the playground. *Liebling*, can you thank
Aunt Lois for taking care of you today?"

"*Danke,*" mumbled the toddler, not raising her head.

"Don't take offense by what I've said," her uncle said,

rising and patting Hannah on the head. "But think it over."

Emma went outdoors and gently placed Hannah in the high-wheeled cart, where the still-wakening child snuggled down on the cushion. Then she walked the quarter mile back to her cottage, pulling the wagon behind her.

She realized she had transitioned from sad to grumpy. Sad at the loss of her business dreams and grumpy at the sudden pressure to do something she didn't want to do. She didn't want to remarry. She didn't.

Yet, was a lifetime of being single what she really wanted? The empty years stretched before her, stark and solitary. Now that they were middle-aged, her aunt and uncle leaned on each other for strength, support, mutual affection and day-to-day activities. Could she do things by herself for the rest of her life? Did she want to?

She thought about how Hannah's face lit up whenever she saw Thomas. She realized her own affections had been captured by the man…but to the point of getting married? She didn't know.

Besides, there was still that mystery about his past, the past he never spoke of and deliberately avoided. Until he came clean, she wasn't sure she could entertain serious thoughts about a courtship with him.

But would fear keep her from missing the opportunity of a lifetime?

"Park?" asked Hannah suddenly as they approached the cabin.

"Not today," replied Emma. "Tomorrow, remember?"

"Ja." Recovered from her nap, the child gave a little bounce in the wagon. "Swing!"

"Ja, I can push you on the swing. And you can help me pack a picnic basket and we'll have a picnic, too, okay?"

"Ja!" The child's shout echoed off the trees. Emma smiled at her little daughter's enthusiasm.

The clock ticked toward Thomas's regular lunchtime. The Yoders insisted he take a full hour off each day, but often he ate lunch at his desk since he usually didn't have anything else to do.

Today, he'd decided to treat himself to one of the excellent hamburgers at a nearby diner. "I'm off to lunch," he called to Mabel, who was busy helping a customer. She waved a hand in acknowledgment.

Thomas plopped his straw hat on his head and stepped outside onto the broad porch of the mercantile. The Yoders had put out a display of mums and some gourds, since fall was on its way. He glanced at a few of the tall oaks and maples located in the city park three blocks away, wondering when their leaves would change color.

Then his eyes narrowed. He recognized Emma pulling the handle of the wagon with the oversized wheels from even three blocks away. She was a neat figure in her dark green dress and black apron. Hannah was in the wagon, pointing around at things excitedly. Emma stopped in front of the park and lifted the child out of the wagon, and Hannah instantly darted for the playground. Emma followed at a more sedate pace.

Suddenly, Thomas knew what he was going to do during his lunch hour. He walked down the porch steps of the mercantile and strode toward the park.

He wanted to know what lay underneath Emma's determination—almost desperation—to secure a loan for the store. It struck him that Mabel's theory was likely correct. But it was something he wanted to verify from Emma herself.

He walked across the street and ambled along the sidewalk. He saw Emma remove a basket from the wagon and begin to spread items on a picnic table. Hannah romped in a small section of the playground designed for very young children.

The park was a cool and shady oasis from the bright early-autumn sun. Emma didn't see him until he was very close. *"Guder nammidaag."*

She whirled and he saw surprise on her face. She pressed a hand to her chest. "Goodness, you startled me. *Guder nammidaag.*"

"Mr. Thomas!" Hannah squealed. The toddler dashed from the play area and launched herself at him. He chuckled and lifted the child, who threw her arms around his neck. At her tiny embrace, Thomas realized how lonely he was and how much he wanted children.

"A picnic looks like fun," he observed.

"Ja. I promised Hannah yesterday that if she was a *gut* girl while my aunt watched her, I'd take her to the playground."

"How are you doing?"

She seemed to understand exactly what he meant. "Still frosted," she admitted, turning to remove some more items from the hamper. "But my uncle took me to task for trying to talk the Yoders into cosigning a loan."

"Gut."

Hannah squirmed to get down, so Thomas set her on the ground and she dashed for the play structure. She didn't have any trouble scaling the wide steps leading to the slides and brightly colored activities. There were chimes played with a padded mallet hanging from a cord and an oversized tic-tac-toe board that could be flipped to reveal amusing illustrations.

"Did you come here to gloat?" Emma inquired with some asperity.

"Actually, I came over to see how you're doing after yesterday's disappointment."

She sighed. "Have some lunch. I have plenty," she invited. "You can use the plate I brought for Hannah."

"Danke." He took the plate and filled it with a scoop of chicken potpie and potato salad and then paused for a brief blessing.

He wondered how to broach the subject of her intense disappointment over the business loan, and decided on bluntness. "Mabel said something interesting after you left the store yesterday," he began.

"What?"

"I said something along the lines of how driven you are to open this store, despite my impression you're doing fairly well financially. Mabel just about clunked me upside the head and said the explanation was simple. It's because you are a single mother and must not only be a single parent to Hannah, but be the only breadwinner as well."

Emma looked like she had swallowed a hedgehog. She choked a bit on a bite of food, swallowed and looked grumpy. "Maybe Mabel is right."

"That's what I wanted to ask you."

She sighed and laid down her fork. "I suppose it's no secret what happened with my first husband. You may as well hear the story."

"Only if you're ready to tell me. In the end, it really isn't my business." But he did want to know what had happened to her. Badly.

She shrugged and didn't meet his eyes. "Maybe if you hear about my past, you'll understand why I hold the…the unconventional position of wanting to remain a single mother."

"I'll admit I'm curious," he said cautiously.

She glanced up at him. "And *I'll* admit to being interested in you, Thomas. Part of it has to do with my daughter's uncanny affection for you straight off the bat. But you should understand what I went through before Hannah was even born. It left a mental scar with me that still hurts."

"You said you got pregnant with her out of wedlock, *ja*?"

"*Ja*, and that was just the start of a cascade of failures that could've—had not *Gott* seen to answer my prayers—resulted in me being miserable the rest of my life. But *Gott did* answer my prayers, and now my husband is dead."

Thomas was staggered by that statement. "D-do you mean to say you prayed for your *hutband*'s death?" he stuttered.

"Of course not," she replied tartly. "I prayed to be released from my marriage. Somehow. Since marriage in our church is until 'death do us part,' some may argue it's the same thing. But I can assure you, it never crossed my mind to wish him dead."

Thomas chose his words carefully. "It sounds like he wasn't a *gut* match for you."

She made a distasteful expression. "That's putting it mildly. He hadn't been baptized and, to be honest, I couldn't see him ever becoming so. He was arrogant, *hochmut*. He belittled me at every opportunity. I know it was just his method to prop up a weak ego, but since I was vulnerable and pregnant at the time, I took his criticism to heart more than I should have."

"And…" Again, Thomas was careful to phrase things delicately. "And you married him solely because you were pregnant?"

"*Ja*. He was very handsome and—and I guess *char-*

ismatic is the right word. In the height of adolescence, sometimes that's all that matters. It just took one mistake and, within six weeks, I knew that mistake was permanent. We were pressured to make a commitment I didn't want."

"The proverbial shotgun wedding, *ja*?"

"*Ja*, something like that. And though it was only four years ago, I was so immature at the time. I was scared and confused and didn't know anything else except to go along with it."

His eyebrows twitched together in concern. "Did your parents force you?"

"*Nein*, not really. I think they were disappointed in me, but I don't think they would have forced me. However, our bishop in Indiana was made of sterner stuff, and he basically convinced both Simeon and me that the only honorable course of action was to marry. I'd had a sinking feeling that would be a mistake, and it was. I prayed for a way out. The vows I took in church seemed like a mockery. 'Is it ordained of *Gott* to be thy wedded *hutband...*' That's part of the vows that were said, but it's not how I felt. So, I suppose you might say I lied. Lied during my own wedding ceremony. But what else could I do?"

"And he was not baptized?"

"*Nein*. Neither was I at the time, so we were never shunned."

"I'm surprised you were married in the church."

"I think the assumption was we would both be baptized afterward. There was no time beforehand." She scrubbed a hand over her face. "It was such an awful time..."

"So what happened during the marriage? Was he abusive?"

"*Nein*. He never hit me. But he was hateful. He didn't

want the marriage any more than I did. He probably felt just as trapped as I did, and there was a baby on the way. He was reckless and rebellious, much more so after we got married. He had a car he'd bought when he was on his *rumspringa*, and he drove it too fast. I hated being in the car with him because I always felt he would crash it. Well, he did, but by the grace of *Gott*, I wasn't with him at the time."

Thomas spoke thoughtfully. "I suppose I can understand your sense of relief when he died."

"*Ja*. And it makes me feel guilty to be relieved. Who knows? He might have grown out of his rebellion. But suddenly, I was without him, back living with my parents. Two months later, Hannah was born, and I was glad she didn't have to grow up with a father like that."

"How long ago did you come to Montana?"

"About a year and a half ago. There were just too many bad memories in my hometown. When Uncle Samuel and Aunt Lois invited me to come here, I jumped at the chance. They've been very *gut* to me, standing in the stead of my parents."

"Do you get along with your parents?"

"Oh, *ja*! They're wonderful people. I miss them a lot." Emma picked at the crust of the chicken potpie. "I sometimes wonder if seeing them so happy in their marriage while I was growing up was detrimental. Because how could I ever find someone I could be as happy with? It seemed impossible. That said, I should never have risked my future with Simeon."

"You seem like such a *gut* mother to Hannah."

Emma glanced over at her daughter on the playground and her face took on a soft glow. "I love that child more than life itself. I would die if something happened to her."

At that moment, Hannah tripped over her own feet

and fell. Thomas saw Emma tense, but she didn't rush to cluck over the child. Instead, she let the toddler climb to her own feet and understand she was unhurt. Sure enough, Hannah came over to the picnic table. "I fell, *Mamm.*"

"So I saw. And then you were brave and got up. Would you like some chicken pie, *liebling*?"

"*Ja!* Hungry." Distracted, the child appeared to forget all about her tumble.

Thomas nodded. Emma understood it was best not to cater to a weakness or failure, but instead to work through it. In a larger sense, she had done the exact same thing with her own life. He admired the strength she had developed as a result.

Emma lifted the toddler into her lap and tucked a napkin over her dress. She gave Hannah a fork, which the child tried her best to eat with. She was mostly successful, though some ended up on Emma as well.

To Thomas, her love for the child was painted all over her. He had seen mothers with their children hundreds of times, but there was something about Emma's natural aptitude that struck him as profound. Or perhaps he was mentally casting her in a role he wanted but she didn't.

But whatever vague hopes he placed on this woman, they weren't likely to come to fruition. It wasn't just her determination to stay single. It was also his own heavy past. There was no way she would ever consider someone like him if she knew what he had been like until only a year ago. He didn't dare pin hopes on this strong and wonderful woman.

He hid his chaotic thoughts with a sad smile. "So what I'm concluding from all this is I don't have a hope of ever courting you, is that it?"

Her shrug seemed defensive. "*Ja.* I think so. I'm scared,

Thomas. Scared of making another mistake. I was nearly given a life sentence, yoked with a man I did not love. With him gone, I've been happier than I ever was before, even though I'm disappointed over losing the prospect of having my own store. How can I give up that independence?"

"Not that I'm trying to push you into something you're not ready for, but is this a state you'd be happy in for the rest of your life? Think of yourself at your Aunt Lois's age, for example. Only one child, no *hutband*… That's a long time to be alone."

He regretted his words, for she got a bleak look on her face. He could almost see her mind recoiling from the long, empty years ahead.

"I don't know," she said at last, bringing her gaze back to him. "All I know is this decision is right for me, at least for now."

He nodded. "I won't try to talk you out of it. It certainly sounds like you dodged a bullet with Simeon."

"I did." Emma guided a cup toward Hannah's mouth. The child clasped the cup and drank. Then she started wiggling. "Me go play?" she asked.

"*Ja*, go play." Emma put the child back on the ground, and Hannah dashed for the playground again. Her gaze lingered on the child. "There's another thing you should know. When I was being pressured into marrying Simeon, the bishop said something to me. He said I would be a financial drain on the community if I didn't marry the man who got me pregnant. He may have said something similar to Simeon, I don't know. But perhaps those words were more haunting than I realized. Whatever the cause, I've reached a conclusion no one will like."

Thomas felt alarm. "What?"

"That if I'm pressured again to marry when I'm not ready, I'd rather leave the church."

Thomas felt the blood drain from his face. "You can't," he croaked. "You have no idea the implications of that statement."

"It would be better than facing another unwanted marriage." She looked stubborn.

"Emma, think it through. You're baptized. If you left the church, you would be shunned. Do you really think you could succeed as a single mother out in the *Englisch* world without the support of family members or the church community?"

A flicker of uncertainty crossed her face. "Is it worse than what I faced before?"

"*Ja*, much worse! I should know. I spent many years in the *Englisch* world before I came to my senses and came back to the church." He gestured toward the scar on his face. "It can be a hard and cruel place. Besides, this time you're not pregnant and vulnerable. No one's forcing you to do anything."

"Maybe you're right." Her shoulders slumped. "But I'm getting some pressure from Uncle Samuel and Aunt Lois to remarry, and it dredges up all the old fears. I told them yesterday evening that I had no intention of remarrying. They were shocked and urged me to reconsider." She paused and a grim smile played across her lips. "I should warn you, your name came up in the process."

He raised his eyebrows. "I see." A thought occurred to him. "You've never been courted, have you?"

She looked startled. *"Nein,"* she said slowly. "I guess I never have." She toyed with the food on her plate and then suddenly looked up. "Okay, turnabout is fair play. I've told you my deep, dark secrets. Now what about you?

What is it you're hiding in your own past? How did you get that scar on your face?"

Caught off guard, he stared. It was the last thing he'd expected and his mind desperately darted around like a trapped animal.

"You don't want to know," he finally croaked.

"Sure I do."

He closed his eyes for a moment and then opened them and met hers somberly. "I'm sorry, Emma, but I can't tell you."

Chapter Twelve

Emma felt conflicting emotions at Thomas's refusal. Her eyebrows twitched together. "Let me get this straight. I just spilled my guts and you're refusing to reciprocate? Pardon me if I feel just a bit betrayed." She heard the annoyance in her own voice.

The annoyance faded when she saw a look of raw pain flicker across his face. It disappeared so fast, she wondered if she'd imagined it.

No, she hadn't imagined it. When he spoke, his voice was bitter. "*Nein*, you don't want to know," he said. "If you think your deceased *hutband* had issues, it's nothing to what I used to be like."

"You're nothing like my deceased *hutband*."

"Maybe not, but I'm not proud of my past."

"Try me."

"*Nein.*" He gave her a sad smile. "I'm going to have to ask you to trust me when I say I have my reasons for keeping things to myself. All I'll say is I'm humbled by *Gott*'s redeeming grace. It's why I want so badly to be baptized and never look back."

She toyed with her fork, her eyes on her plate. "So it looks like we're both tangled by the messy ties from our pasts. I wonder, can we ever look forward?" Thomas's refusal to trust her with his secrets hurt her more than she was willing to admit. She realized she had, deep down, pinned some false hopes that Thomas could turn into a sort of knight in shining armor who would sweep away the ghosts of her past and make her realize why she didn't have to face her future alone.

But it seemed he had too many ghosts of his own.

"I'm doing nothing *but* looking forward," he replied. "I can't change my past, but I can change my future. It's all I can do." His voice warmed. "There's so much here that I like. There's a *gut* church, a *gut* job, starting my own business, being able to work on building projects. There's so much here for me. Isn't it the same for you? Isn't that why you moved west, to get a new start in life?"

"Ja." She took a bite and swallowed before continuing. "And I have the same reasons as you. Church, community ties. You're right, I couldn't leave that behind. I should be content but…"

"Are you restless?"

"Nein, I don't feel restless. Just…incomplete. Like something's missing."

"A *hutband* and more *kinner*, perhaps?" He quirked a small smile at her.

"Now you sound like Uncle Samuel."

"You're a woman of many contradictions, Emma. First, you say you want to stay single and independent, and then you say you feel incomplete."

"I don't understand it myself." She sighed. "Life is never simple, is it?"

"Nein. But, Emma, there's something you might think about." He toyed with his fork. "I'm sure I've made it clear I would like to court you. Whatever drive you feel

to start a business to provide for Hannah is a burden that can be shared. Think about it."

For whatever reason, the idea startled her. For so long—even before Hannah's birth—her sole focus had been *independence*. It was her coping mechanism after being widowed while still pregnant. But Thomas might have a point. Could burdens be shared?

Before she could gather her thoughts, he glanced at the sun dappling through the trees. "I should probably get back to work. I imagine my lunch hour is nearly over."

"*Ja*, sure." Emma turned to glance at Hannah, who was twirling on a little spinner, preoccupied. She had a smudge on her cheek. "Hannah? *Liebling*, it's time to go. Mr. Thomas has to get back to work."

Emma turned to tuck away the food. Hannah climbed off the spinner and made a beeline for Thomas, who bent to lift her into his arms. He chuckled. "Your hands and face are dirty. I think your *mamm* is going to have to give you a bath when you get home."

Watching how easily he interacted with her child, Emma felt her throat close up. He was so *gut* with her daughter. In fact, he seemed like a *gut* man altogether. Why hadn't he ever married? Did his mysterious past include a woman? She wondered if she would ever learn.

"I'll go with you to the store," she said. "Mabel should have my paycheck ready."

"If you're okay pulling the wagon, I'll carry this little one." He gave Hannah a small bounce.

For the briefest moment, Emma wondered if she was jealous of her daughter's preference for this man...and then she decided she wasn't.

"When is your next day working at the store?" inquired Thomas as he reached the edge of the park and headed for the crosswalk. Yoder's Mercantile was just three blocks away, across the street. He stepped off the curb. "Because it occurs to me you might—"

The roar of an engine interrupted his words. Startled, Emma whipped around and saw an older pickup truck blowing through stop signs at the four-way intersection and bearing down on them at high speed. She caught the barest glimpse of the driver. He looked almost like a child.

She emitted a three-octave scream and dropped the handle of the wagon. In a split second, Thomas turned and literally threw Hannah at her. The weight of the child hitting her made Emma stagger back and lose her footing. She instinctively clasped the back of Hannah's head with one hand to protect her, while her own head slammed into the pavement so hard she saw stars.

Tires screeched. People screamed. She heard a gut-wrenching cry as the truck hit Thomas with a sickening *thud*. His hat was flattened under the vehicle as he went flying over the hood of the truck, hit the windshield, bounced off and slammed onto the street, rolling a few times.

The truck came to a stop a few yards away and the driver slumped over the steering wheel, his face buried in his arms.

Hannah wailed in Emma's arms. Emma tried to crawl to her feet but seemed unable to move. All she could see was Thomas lying on the street, bloodied and absolutely still.

"Oh, *Gott*, don't let him be dead," she prayed. She couldn't move. Why couldn't she move?

Vaguely, she heard shouts and lamentations as people crowded around Thomas. She saw blood on the pavement. Thomas's blood. Several people were on their cell phones, undoubtedly calling for an ambulance.

Things became blurred. Solicitous hands helped her up, patted her baby, supported her, moved her off the street—but she was numb. The only thing that seemed real was Thomas lying still in the road, and Hannah's little body clasped against hers. Emma's arms were locked so tightly around the child that she felt they were frozen in place.

A babble of voices asked if she was okay, asked if the baby was hurt… Emma barely heard or understood anyone. She stared in horror at Thomas, what she could see of him on the street surrounded by anxious citizens.

All she could think was that he was dead—yanked out of her life just as she'd began developing a sincere interest in him. More than that, he'd literally sacrificed his life to save Hannah. "Please, *Gott*, don't let him be dead," she prayed. Her teeth chattered, and her body trembled so hard her knees buckled. Someone helped her sit down on the curb.

There was a scream of sirens and people parted as an ambulance and a police car drove up, lights flashing on both vehicles. The paramedics poured out of the vehicle and swarmed around Thomas. Two police officers approached the driver of the pickup truck.

Hannah still wailed in her arms. Dimly, Emma wondered if she was holding the child too tightly, but her arms seemed locked. An older woman offered her a handkerchief and asked if she wanted her to sop up the blood on the back of her head. Blood? What blood? Emma felt dazed and speechless.

The paramedics slipped a foam collar around Thomas's neck and slid him onto a stretcher. They strapped him in and wheeled the stretcher to the back of the ambulance. Someone pointed at Emma, and one of the paramedics broke away from the others and approached her.

"Ma'am, are you hurt?" he inquired, squatting down before her.

She stared at him, mute, with Hannah still wailing in her locked arms.

"Ma'am?" The paramedic reached out and gently thumped her on the shoulder. "Ma'am, can you answer me?"

"Is—is he d-dead?" Her teeth chattered.

"No, ma'am. But we need to get him immediate medical attention." He eyed her *kapp*. "You too. You've been hurt."

Was she hurt? She didn't feel any pain, except in her arms since she was clutching Hannah so tightly. Was Hannah hurt? Why was there blood on her apron? Why was...

"Can you stand?" inquired the paramedic. "This police officer can escort you to the hospital."

Only then did Emma become aware a second police car had arrived and a uniformed officer stood nearby, watching her.

"*Ja. Danke.* Thank you." She tried to stand, swayed and nearly fell. A choking blackness nearly obliterated her sight. The paramedic leaped to one side and the officer moved to the other. They each took an elbow and half walked, half carried her to the police car. She still clutched Hannah. The child's wails had subsided into terrified hiccups.

The ambulance drove off with its lights flashing. Emma knew the hospital was only a few blocks away in this tiny town.

The paramedic got into the back seat of the police car with Emma and Hannah. The police officer got behind the wheel, pulled a U-turn and drove down the main street of the town, lights flashing too.

Emma leaned her head against the seat back, closed her eyes and prayed.

* * *

Thomas groaned as sharp pain ricocheted through him. He couldn't move. Why couldn't he move?

"Lie still," someone told him. A male voice.

He couldn't move even if he wanted to. He couldn't even open his eyes. He tried to raise an arm, but it felt tied down. He tried to roll over and couldn't. Something heavy and thick seemed to be around his neck.

"Lie still," the unknown man repeated. "We have to examine you for spinal injuries, so try not to move."

Thomas had an impression of the swaying movement of a vehicle and the low chatter of more than one person nearby. An electronic-sounding squawk of a radio voice came from a few feet away, but in his bleary state he couldn't discern where he was.

What happened?

The feeling of movement ceased, he heard some bangs, and he felt something underneath him roll and rattle. His mind cleared enough to realize he was on a gurney being wheeled inside a hospital. Staff members were barking orders around him. Overhead lights swirled in a sickening crescendo.

He blacked out once more.

When he came to, he was in a hospital room. He blinked with bleary eyes, seeing a darkened window—was it night?—and a shadowed room with a sickly green glow of monitors that highlighted a tangle of cords and tubes. He tried to move and the resulting pain was so bad, he caught his breath.

He heard movement nearby. To his astonishment, he saw Emma leaning over his bed, an expression of desperate worry on her face. She had a large bruise on one cheek.

"Wh…" His voice was hoarse.

"Shh," she whispered. "Don't try to talk. I'm going to call the nurse."

She disappeared from his sight and, within a few moments, an older woman in scrubs stepped into his line of sight. She had an encouraging smile.

"I imagine you feel pretty bad right now," the nurse said in a quiet voice.

"Ja," he rasped. "What happened?"

"We'll tell you in a while. But for now, I'm going to give you a sedative to control the pain and let you sleep a bit more. Okay?"

"Ja, okay…" He was hardly in a position to object. He felt a poke on his arm and drifted off.

The next time he swam out of the fog of unconsciousness, the window was gray, as if lit up with predawn light. Emma was slumped in a nearby padded recliner chair, her chin on her chest, fast asleep. The bruise on her cheek looked dark and ominous. Her *kapp* was in place but stained with blood. Her dress and apron were dirty.

He searched his mind, trying to remember what had happened, groping through the mist for clarity. Park. Picnic. Hannah playing on the playground. Emma telling him about her deceased husband. Screams. Cries of horror. Fragments of conversation flickered through his muddled mind as he tried to piece together whatever had occurred to land him in the hospital.

The image of a pickup truck hovered at the edge of his mind. Something about the expression on the driver's face nicked his memory—a look of horror. But more than that, there was something about the driver that seemed familiar. He didn't remember anything that happened next. Had the pickup truck hit him?

His gaze rested on Emma as she slumbered in the chair. Something she'd said earlier came to him. *I love that child more than life itself. I would die if something happened to her...*

Why had those words come back to him? Hannah—where was she? Had he *thrown* the child somewhere? Thrown her at Emma...

He lay there in bed, puzzling over events that were scrambled and confused.

He lifted his arm and felt a tug. He had an IV taped to the back of his hand and he stared at it stupidly. Was he in that bad a shape that he needed an IV?

He looked over at the woman in the chair. "Emma," he croaked.

She woke up instantly, blinking the sleep from her eyes. When she saw him looking at her, she sprang to her feet. "You're awake!"

"Seems that way." He tried to push himself up and winced from the pain.

"Don't try to move. You're probably a mass of bruises, and you don't want to risk any more injuries to your internal organs."

"What happened?" His tongue felt thick.

"Take some ice chips. They'll help." As if he were a child, she spooned some half-melted ice chips into his mouth. "You were hit by a car. Well, a pickup truck."

He sucked at the chips and felt fractionally improved. "So, it wasn't a dream."

"Nein." She hesitated. "How much do you remember?"

"Bits and pieces. My brain feels very thick." He paused. "What's wrong with me?"

"The doctor said you have a couple of cracked ribs and massive amounts of bruising. He was worried about your internal organs being bruised, as well, so he's watching for that. You also have a hairline fracture in your skull."

He tried to smile, but even that was painful. "No wonder everything hurts."

"I have a feeling you're going to be here for a while."

"Abe and Mabel won't be happy…"

"Abe and Mabel got by without you for a long time. They can manage another couple of weeks. Oh, Thomas, everyone has been so worried…" She buried her face in her apron and broke down crying.

Thomas couldn't even reach out to comfort her in her grief. "I'll be fine, Emma…" he managed to say.

"It's more than that," she sobbed. "You saved Hannah's life. Do you remember what happened? You threw her right at me just before the truck hit you. If you hadn't done that, she would have been killed. I've been so worried about you." Her shoulders heaved.

So, it hadn't been a dream—throwing Hannah. "Is she okay?"

"Ja." Emma sniffed and wiped her eyes. "She was scared and got a bruise or two, but she's fine. They checked her out here in the emergency room, and then she went home with Aunt Lois and Uncle Samuel." She sniffed, fished a handkerchief out of her apron pocket and mopped her face.

"Your face has a bruise, and is that blood on your *kapp*?" he asked. "Do you get hurt too?"

"Only because catching Hannah sent me flying backward and I cracked my head on the street. The truck missed us entirely. All I got was some scrapes and a small head cut. Because I got a nasty headache later on, the doctor had to make sure I didn't have a concussion. But I'll be okay. It's *you* I'm worried about."

"Well, I'm awake," he tried to joke. "That's half the battle. I imagine the guy driving the pickup is in trouble, though."

"It was a kid. A police officer told me," she said. "A teenager that doesn't even have his driver's license. *Ja*, I expect he's in a lot of trouble."

"I wonder…" His tongue felt thick. "Was it Jeremy?"

"Who's Jeremy?"

"Remember that *youngie* who shoplifted in the grocery store? The one I caught in the park trying to set fire to the garbage cans? His name is Jeremy."

"*Ja*, I remember now you mention it. But I don't know the name of the driver."

A nurse peeked in the doorway. "You're awake," she exclaimed in delight. "Good morning."

"Good morning." Thomas smiled wanly. "What time is it?"

"About six in the morning. You slept the night through, which is wonderful." The nurse came into the room, peered at a monitor and wrote something down on a clipboard. Then she looked at Emma. "And Miss Fisher, how do you feel?"

"A little sore, but otherwise okay."

The nurse nodded. "Good. The doctor will be checking up on both of you during his morning rounds."

"How long do I have to stay in the hospital?" asked Thomas.

"It's not up to me to say, but probably no more than a couple days. You probably don't feel ready to leave anyway."

Thomas assessed his sore body and nodded. "*Ja*, you're right. At the moment, the last thing I think I could do is sit at a desk, much less swing a hammer."

The nurse chuckled. "If you haven't lost your sense of humor, you'll be fine. Are either of you hungry? I can have the cafeteria send something up."

Thomas didn't feel like eating. He started to shake

his head but the pain stopped him. "*Nein*. No," he said instead.

"Me, either," added Emma. "Right now, I think I would choke if I tried to eat something. Although I wouldn't mind a cup of tea."

"Tea it is. And for you?" the nurse asked Thomas.

"*Ja*, please." Hot tea actually sounded wonderful.

After the nurse left, Thomas looked at Emma. "Did you stay here the whole night?"

"*Ja*. They wanted to monitor me, as well, so I convinced them to let me keep vigil on you." Tears welled up in her eyes again. "You saved Hannah's life. I had to stay."

Thomas was touched more than he dared admit. "I'll be fine, Emma," he said gently. "I'm just grateful to *Gott* this wasn't worse, and that you and Hannah are okay."

"Thanks to you. You're a hero, Thomas."

It was all he could to do to keep from snorting in derision. A *hero* was the last thing he considered himself to be. Not after years of being a criminal.

But if he was a *hero* in Emma's eyes, who was he to argue? Maybe she would be willing to overlook his decidedly unheroic past after this.

Could he take the chance and tell her about the person he used to be?

Chapter Thirteen

Thomas slept most of that first day and night in the hospital. By the second day, he was feeling better—sore, but more coherent.

The doctor was pleased with his progress. "I see no reason why we can't discharge you in a couple of days," he told Thomas. "With strict orders to minimize exertion." A look of curiosity came over the doctor's face. "I'm not overly familiar with Amish culture. Do you normally travel by horse and buggy?"

"*Ja*, that's common," explained Thomas. "But I'm new in town and don't own one. I'm staying at the Miller's boardinghouse and ride a bike when visiting people in the settlement. Or I walk, of course."

The doctor rubbed his chin. "Your mobility might be limited for a while," he said. "Riding a bike is out of the question, and while walking is fine, I suggest you limit yourself to short distances only."

"Fortunately, my workplace is just a couple blocks from the boardinghouse."

"Where do you work?"

"Yoder's Mercantile. I'm their new bookkeeper."

He nodded. "Your brain will feel scrambled for a couple more days, but once you feel ready to start handling numbers again, I see no reason why you can't work a couple of hours a day. But you'll tire easily and won't be able to concentrate for more than that, at least at first. I can write a note to your employers explaining that, if you like."

"I'm sure that won't be necessary, but I'll let you know if I need it."

The doctor smiled. "I think I'll be able to discharge you as early as tomorrow. You might need to make arrangements to have someone drive you back to your boardinghouse, or perhaps I can arrange for a car…"

"I'm sure my landlord would pick me up. He gives me rides to our church service held in the settlement."

"That's good, then. This could have been much worse," the doctor told Thomas. "And from what I understand, you saved the baby's life by throwing her at her mother just before you got hit. That took bravery."

Thomas wasn't used to praise. "Believe me, Doctor, it was pure instinct," he said. "I like to think it was *Gott* who took over. It certainly wasn't me."

"I'm willing to give God the credit too," said the doctor. "Because everyone will recover. Including you."

The doctor smiled and departed, and then the visitors began.

Abe and Mabel Yoder poked their heads in the door. *"Guder mariye!"* they said in unison.

Thomas was delighted to see them. "Did you bring my ledgers?" he joked.

Abe drew up chairs for both himself and his wife. "Everyone's been so worried about you," he said. "They wouldn't let us visit yesterday. They said you were sleeping."

"And so I was. I actually feel better today." He explained what the doctor had said about reduced working hours.

Mabel looked almost horrified. "We don't expect you'll be able to work for quite some time," she told him. "The last thing we want to do is put you to work before you're ready. It might slow your recovery."

Abe nodded. "You take as long as you need to get well. That's the only important thing."

Thomas was touched by their concern. "To be honest, I'll probably be so bored with nothing to do that I'll look forward to some work. But I understand what the doctor said about my brain feeling scrambled. When it unscrambles itself, I'll come in for an hour or two and see what happens."

His next visitor was the bishop. "You have been getting many, many prayers," began the older man. "Are they working?"

Thomas managed to chuckle. "I think so, *ja*. I can feel myself mending." He explained what the doctor had said about his work schedule and limited exercise. "I don't know that I'll be at this Sunday's church service," he concluded.

The bishop waved a hand dismissively. "*Gott* can be heard just as easily from a hospital room. Thomas…" The church leader trailed off and a suspicious hint of moisture appeared in his eyes. "You likely saved the lives of my niece and grandniece. *Gott* has His hand on you."

Thomas didn't expect this kind of emotional gratitude. He was almost uncomfortable being the object of praise. "It was the hand of *Gott*," he told the bishop.

"I believe it was. But this old man is more grateful than I can say."

The next visitor was one of the police officers who had

responded to the scene, Marcus Gonzales. "How are you feeling?" he asked, shaking Thomas's hand.

"Still a bit banged up, but I'm feeling better," Thomas replied. "I'm glad to see you. Can you tell me everything that happened?"

Officer Gonzales pulled up a chair and explained how a teenager had taken his parents' pickup truck and gone on a joyride. "He doesn't have a license and had no business getting behind the wheel of that truck," explained the officer. "The kid is in a world of trouble."

Thomas remembered the vague familiarity of the face behind the wheel. "The teen... What's his name?"

"Jeremy Watson," replied the officer. "Why?"

Thomas was fairly certain the accident had been caused by the same teen he'd caught in an act of arson. He refrained from mentioning that incident to the officer. "What will happen to him?"

"Probation, for the moment," said the officer. "And doubtless a fine." The man shook his head. "Even a town as small as this has its share of juvenile delinquents. I hope this kid finds a way to straighten himself out."

The officer visited for a few more minutes and then departed. Thomas leaned back in bed and thought about Jeremy Watson. And he wondered...

Last year, when his brother sacrificed himself financially to hire a lawyer to clear Thomas of the charges of involuntary manslaughter, he had promised to pay back the money, but his brother hadn't let him. Joseph had said, "Don't. Pay it forward instead. Someday, you're going to come across someone who needs help. Pay off your debt to me by helping them."

Ever since then, that conversation had hovered at the back of his mind. He was anxious to fulfill that promise, to do an act of kindness that might have the same life-changing impact as he had experienced. What better way to pay it forward than to help a kid avoid the life of petty crime that Thomas had left behind?

Thomas didn't know anything about this teenager except his home life wasn't ideal and he was taking out his adolescent frustrations with increasing levels of dangerous behavior. But the boy had also expressed an interest in learning carpentry.

Thomas recalled when Adam Chupp, the project foreman on the house building a couple of weeks ago, had indicated he was looking to hire. He'd said he might even try contacting the local high school to see if he could hire a kid and train him.

Was this the answer? Was this *Gott*'s way of letting Thomas know he could pay it forward by connecting Jeremy Watson with Adam?

He didn't know, but it seemed a clear doorway. He needed to find some way to get hold of Jeremy Watson, some way to…

His thoughts were interrupted by a soft knock on the doorframe. Emma poked her head inside. She carried Hannah in one arm and a basket in the other.

He was delighted to see them both. *"Guder mariye."*

Emma was dressed in a dark blue dress and clean apron. The bruise on her cheek was fading into a sickly combination of yellows and greens, but she was still beautiful, and her smile lit up the room.

She put Hannah down and the child darted for the hospital bed. "Hi! Hi!" she cried.

The toddler tried to climb up on the bed, but Emma put the basket on the floor and stopped her. *"Nein, liebling.* Mr. Thomas still doesn't feel well. Here, you can sit in this chair." She placed one of the guest chairs next to the bed.

Thomas reached out his hand that didn't have the IV taped to it and chucked Hannah under the chin. "How are you, *liebling*? Did you get hurt in that nasty accident?"

"Nein," the child said solemnly. She looked up at him with big brown eyes. "But *Mamm* got hurt."

Thomas glanced at Emma's cheek. "Your *mamm* was brave, wasn't she?"

"Ja."

"I brought you something." Emma hefted the basket onto the bedside table and began unpacking it. There was a bundle of spearmint and a bouquet of flowers.

"Like candy," announced Hannah, pointing to the pungent herb. "I picked them."

There was also a bar of pine-scented soap and some freshly baked cookies.

"Wow!" Thomas was touched. He couldn't remember the last time someone had given him gifts…with the exception, of course, of the ultimate gift his brother had given him last year—his freedom.

He picked up the spearmint and crushed a leaf to release the smell. "It makes this stale hospital room smell so much better."

"Now, tell me who has come to see you today." Emma drew up a chair next to Hannah.

Thomas related the information from all his visitors, including the police officer. "He confirmed the name of the driver in the pickup truck," he concluded. "And, yes, I'm pretty sure it's the same kid I saw in the park. I wish I could see him."

Emma looked confused. "Why?"

Thomas could hardly explain his quest to pay it forward, not when Emma was unfamiliar with his past. He prevaricated. "He seems like a troubled kid. I just feel this urge to help him."

"I'm sure the police officer might be able to get hold of him. Now, tell me what the doctor said."

"He thinks I can be out of here, maybe as early as tomorrow. I may have to ask Matthew Miller to come pick me up, though. I don't know if I can walk all the way back to the boardinghouse."

"I'll check with Matthew. If he can't, I can borrow Uncle Samuel's horse and buggy and pick you up myself."

"You would do that?"

Emma looked at him. "You saved my daughter's life," she said simply. "I'm in your debt."

In your debt. Yes, she was in Thomas's debt for saving Hannah's life—and she didn't mind in the least. She was willing to do anything for him—pick him up from the hospital, bring him homemade treats, floof his pillow... The precious child sitting next to Thomas chattering about the garden was worth it.

She shuddered to think where Hannah would be now if Thomas hadn't thrown her clear of the truck. Emma might be planning a funeral, not visiting a hospital room.

She couldn't tell Thomas right now—not when he was still recovering—but she had done some hard soul-searching since the accident and had come to an important conclusion. She would welcome courtship from him. A man who was literally willing to sacrifice his life for her daughter was not a man to turn down. Whatever his mysterious past, his solid and reassuring *present* was all that mattered.

A cautious part of her also knew she should wait for the shock of the accident to subside to make sure she was looking at the issue coolly and rationally. Her emotions were still too high and she didn't want to make such an important decision lightly.

Besides, Thomas was lying in bed—his body battered and bruised, his mind still scrambled—and she knew it was not the time to confess this to him. It wouldn't hurt to wait just a little longer.

Meanwhile, she wanted to assure him his medical needs would be taken care of. "Yes, just let me know when you're being released and I'll arrange to get you back to the boardinghouse."

"Danke." His smile was somewhat strained. "Right now, I can't imagine walking the distance to get there. It's less than a mile, but just the thought is ex…exhausting…"

To her alarm, his eyes closed and he appeared to have drifted off to sleep. She stared at him, horrified. Was this normal? Was he okay? She quietly scooped Hannah off the chair and fled out of his room to the nurses' station down the hallway.

"We were talking and he just fell asleep," she babbled to the nurse manning the station. "Is that okay? Is he okay?"

The nurse smiled reassuringly. "Oh, yes, it's quite normal. I'll step over and check his vitals, but don't let it worry you. Also, he's had a number of visitors today, so they might simply have worn him out."

The nurse skirted around the workstation and strode toward Thomas's room with Emma trailing in her wake. The nurse checked the numbers on the monitor, watched Thomas's quiet breathing for a few moments, and came away. She gestured that they should speak outside his room.

"Yes, he's fine," the nurse said. "Just tired. An accident like he experienced, especially coupled with a head injury, takes some time to recuperate from. He's making remarkable progress, but he's not ready to go home yet."

"I guess we should go, then." Emma bounced Hannah gently on her hip. "No sense waiting around with a toddler."

"What a cutie." The nurse touched Hannah's miniature *kapp*. "I have a granddaughter about the same age. I'll let Mr. Kemp know what happened—that he fell asleep and you had to leave."

"*Danke*. Thank you. I'll just go fetch my basket and then I'll be gone."

The nurse walked back to her station. Emma lifted Hannah off her hip and placed her on the floor. "Wait here, *liebling*. I won't be a moment."

"*Ja, Mamm.*"

Emma tiptoed back into Thomas's room. He still slumbered. She picked up her empty basket, hesitated a moment, and then approached him and dropped a kiss on his forehead. "*Danke,*" she whispered to him.

Then she retrieved her daughter and left the hospital.

Her little pull-along wagon with the large wheels stood where she had left it outside the hospital entry. "*Komm, liebling*, I think it's time to make a few stops, and then we'll visit Aunt Lois and Uncle Samuel," she said, lifting the child into the wagon.

"Mr. Thomas *komm* too?"

"He needs to stay in the hospital another couple of days. You be sure to keep saying prayers that he'll get better, *ja*?"

"*Ja.*" The child popped her eyes closed and a look of concentration crossed her face.

Emma chuckled at her daughter's nascent faith. She nestled the basket into the wagon and started back through town.

Her first stop was the boardinghouse to talk to Matthew Miller, the proprietor.

Matthew was checking in some guests. He nodded a greeting, so Emma and Hannah lingered in the lobby until he had shown the guests to their room.

He returned to the lobby with a look of concern on his face. "How's Thomas?" he asked without preamble.

"Improving," she assured him. She filled him in on what the doctor had said.

Matthew closed his eyes and pinched the bridge of his nose. *"Danke, Gott,"* he muttered.

"Ja, I feel the same way. I came by to ask, when it comes time for him to be released from the hospital, would you be able to pick him up with your buggy? He won't be able to walk from the hospital to here. I'd be happy to cover the front desk for you."

"Ja, sure. I'd be happy to. And, *ja*, the people I just checked in will be staying a few days, so if you can man the desk while I pick Thomas up, I'd be grateful."

"Gut. That's one task done. Next I'm going to go talk to Abe and Mabel and see if they can provide meals for him. I'll offer to pay for them. He'll be staying in his room for a few days, so maybe they can deliver."

"I assume it will be some time before he can go back to work?"

"A few days at least, and even then, he may not be able to concentrate for more than a couple hours at a time."

"Recuperating from an accident of that scope will take time." Matthew gave her a narrow look. "You're worried about him, aren't you?"

Emma hoped she wouldn't blush. *"Ja*, of course. And since he saved Hannah's life, I figure the least I can do is make his recovery as easy as possible."

He nodded. "Well, let me know what else I can do."

"Picking him up from the hospital is a huge start. Okay, I'll go talk to the Yoders next."

Emma reloaded Hannah into the wagon, crossed the street and made her way to the mercantile.

She cornered Mable and explained her idea of paying

for Thomas's meals while he recuperated. "Just things he can get here in the store, I mean," added Emma, "pastries, sandwiches, soup, that kind of thing."

"*Ach*, we can cover that," Mabel began.

Emma shook her head. "You're already doing enough by accommodating his work schedule. How about if I bring in items to sell, but rather than log them into my account, I trade them for food? I have a batch of lemon soap ready to go, for example."

"*Ja*, sure, if you like. And I can arrange for one of our *kinner* to bring food to the boardinghouse and drop it off for him."

"*Danke.* I was going to ask. That would be wonderful."

Mabel gave her the same assessing look Matthew Miller had just used a few minutes before. Emma knew the same thought was going through their minds. It must seem to them that her behavior was more like that of a courting woman rather than just another church member.

Emma found she didn't care. Thomas had saved Hannah's life. She would do whatever it took to ease his recovery.

Satisfied with her efforts so far, she started on the long walk back to the Amish settlement three miles outside of town. Hannah, lulled by the movement of the wagon, fell asleep on the padded cushion.

Emma bypassed her own cabin and continued the extra quarter-mile distance to her aunt and uncle's. She found the older couple relaxing on the porch.

"*Ach*, there's my *liebling*." Lois reached out from her chair to take a sleepy Hannah into her lap. The child cuddled against the woman and dozed again.

Emma told her relations about her efforts on Thomas's behalf. "So, Matthew Miller will pick him up from the hospital. He'll probably stay in his room at the boardinghouse for a couple days, so one of the Yoders will bring him meals."

Samuel nodded at these arrangements. "This is very proactive of you, *liebling*. By the grace of *Gott*, it sounds like he'll recover physically. The entire church community will join in to make sure he gets back on his feet in every other respect."

Lois gave Emma a sympathetic look. "I know you are worried about him, *geliebte*. But is there something more?"

Emma knew she could trust her aunt's and uncle's discretion. "*Ja*, maybe there is. I might be wary of my last experience in marriage, but I keep wondering if *Gott* is telling me something about Thomas. He's a respectable man."

"You don't know *how* respectable," said Samuel with an emphasis she didn't understand.

"What do you mean?" she asked, puzzled.

Samuel gave a little shake of his head and adopted a rueful smile. "Never mind. But I'm glad you hold a high opinion of him."

Emma headed home shortly after with Hannah more awake and looking around as she sat in the wagon. She puzzled over her uncle's words. *You don't know how respectable.* What did he know that she didn't?

It was clear that in the short time since Thomas had come to stay in the church settlement, he had built a good reputation. It was something her deceased husband had never achieved.

Maybe she was still riding high on emotion, but she couldn't see anything on the horizon that would make her doubt Thomas's potential as a future *hutband*.

Chapter Fourteen

$\sim$

Thomas improved enormously over the next two days. The soreness faded. His headaches retreated. He felt a bit stiff but attributed that to lack of exercise. He started chafing at being confined to his hospital room.

"The doctor is just being cautious," one of the nurses told him with a smile when he suggested it was time to go home. "That's why he decided to keep you here an extra day. But I must say, you're looking much better."

"Except for being a little stiff, I feel pretty much back to normal." Thomas's clothes had been laundered, and it felt good to be out of the hospital gown and back into regular garments. "Now I'm bored."

"There's always television…" The nurse regarded his Amish apparel and corrected herself with a smile. "We have a small library, or perhaps you'd like to write some letters?"

"Ja." Thomas smiled. "I owe my brother and sister a letter. If you have pen and paper, I can write."

He also requested a Bible. He needed something solid to pass the time.

His stream of visitors hadn't stopped. It was one of the things he loved about the church community. They

were diligent about visiting the sick. In between enter-
taining callers who came to wish him well and check
his recovery, Thomas sat at a small table in front of the
hospital room window and composed a lengthy letter
to his brother, Joseph, explaining everything that had
happened so far. He touched on his romantic interest in
Emma but didn't go much beyond that. And, of course,
he filled Joseph in on his accident and emphasized his
nearly complete recovery.

But the primary point he wanted to make to his brother
was how he might have found a means to pay forward the
debt he felt he owed Joseph for his earthly salvation. He
finished his letter with a chatty description of the town
and surroundings. Then he addressed the envelope and
started another letter to his sister, Miriam.

He was interrupted by another visitor, which confirmed his suspicion that *Gott* was guiding him on how
to pay off his debt. His visitor was Adam Chupp, the
construction company owner.

"Thomas." Adam stepped forward, hand outstretched.
"You look much better than I expected. To be honest, I
feared the worst."

Thomas rose and shook Adam's hand. "*Gut* to see
you. *Ja*, if you'd visited me even yesterday, I would have
looked the part. I could barely get out of bed. But today
I'm feeling much better and champing at the bit to get
out of here." He gestured toward his letters. "I'm pass-
ing the time by writing to my brother and sister. I'm glad
you came," he said. "I wanted to talk to you. Please, sit
down." He pointed at the opposing chair.

Adam looked a bit surprised as he sank down into the
chair. "What did you want to talk to me about?"

"Are you still looking for a young kid to train in your
company?"

"*Ja*, always. Why?"

"Because I might have someone in mind."

Without delving into why Jeremy Watson's youthful transgressions struck a personal chord with him, Thomas explained how he had seen the boy shoplift something from the Yoders and stopped him from his arson experiment in the park, which is where the teen had blurted out an interest in learning construction.

"To top it off," he told the skeptical-looking Adam, "he's the one who was illegally driving the pickup truck that hit me. In short, this kid needs straightening out, and I can think of no finer way than to teach him a trade to keep his hands and mind occupied. *Especially* since he mentioned his interest in learning carpentry."

Adam's eyebrows drew together in a look of concern. "I don't know, Thomas…" He hesitated. "Taking on a juvenile delinquent is not what I had in mind when it came to hiring and training someone. Is bringing a troubled kid with a history of trying to commit arson into a facility that works with wood worth the risk?" He shook his head. "Sounds like a recipe for disaster."

Thomas had set up the perfect redemption opportunity so thoroughly in his mind that Adam's reluctance caught him by surprise. Perhaps he shouldn't have started off with a list of the boy's transgressions. If Adam preferred not to hire the youth, Thomas didn't know what else he could do to help turn the teen around.

He clasped and unclasped his hands and decided on honesty. "I can't vouch for him," he admitted. "And on the surface, you're right. It sounds like a recipe for disaster. But it might be this kid's chance at redemption. He sounds like he has a rough home life. If he were offered the chance of learning a trade and earning some honest money, something tells me it would be a game changer for him."

"But what if the opposite happens? What if he turns to thievery or commits acts of vandalism while under my employ? I would be responsible." Adam shook his head. "It worries me, Thomas."

"I think this kid needs a second chance," Thomas argued and then reluctantly conceded. "But that's easy for me to say when I'm not the one who would be employing him."

What could he do? Thomas could hardly insist Adam fall in with his little fantasy of rescuing a kid who—Thomas had to admit—he'd only spoken to once for five minutes. He could fully understand Adam not wanting to accept the responsibility or potential liability for employing a teenager with such a questionable history.

But he'd been given a second chance in life, and he desperately wanted Jeremy to have that second chance too.

Adam stayed a few minutes longer, exchanged pleasantries, and then left with best wishes for a continuing recovery. After he had gone, Thomas sat in somewhat of a dark funk, staring blindly out the hospital window where some oaks showed a leaf or two that were already changing into fall colors. His perfect solution for Jeremy had turned out to be not so perfect after all.

Had he misinterpreted what he thought *Gott* had wanted when it came to paying forward his debt? Was Jeremy the wrong person to focus on? He couldn't blame Adam for his caution. He himself had been a poor risk only a year ago, yet look at him now.

He didn't have enough income yet for Jeremy to come work for him as a bookkeeper, and the boy hadn't expressed the slightest interest in that field. So how was

Thomas to help if he couldn't offer the kid a distraction against his destructive course?

"You look like a thundercloud is over your head," observed a voice from the doorway.

He turned and saw Emma carrying Hannah. He smiled. "Sorry. I didn't hear you come in."

"Hi! Hi!" Little Hannah wiggled out of her mother's arms and dashed across the room.

Thomas chuckled. The kid was like a ray of sunshine. "*Guder nammidaag*, little one." Carefully, he pulled the child onto his lap.

"You look better." Emma came into the room.

"I feel better. Getting antsy. The doctor said I can be discharged tomorrow."

Her face lit up. "That's *gut*! Matthew said he'll be happy to pick you up and bring you back to the boarding-house." Uninvited, she dropped into the chair so recently vacated by Adam. "Now, what were you thinking about as we came in? As I said, you looked like a thundercloud was over your head."

"Oh." Thomas scrubbed a hand over his face. "Adam Chupp was here…"

"*Ja*, we passed him downstairs in the lobby. He said he came to visit you."

"*Ja*, it was nice of him to *komm*. But I proposed something to him and he wasn't overly enthusiastic about it. I suggested the kid who hit me in his truck, Jeremy Watson, might be a *gut* prospect as a young apprentice carpenter. Adam disagreed because of Jeremy's history."

"Can you blame him? The kid sounds like he's trouble."

"*Nein*. I can't blame him at all. It's a lot to ask. You walked in just as I was trying to figure out another way to help."

"Thomas…" Emma hesitated and then plunged on.

"Why is it so important to you to help this *youngie*? He's not your responsibility. You don't know anything about him except that he expressed a momentary interest in carpentry. I agree with Adam. It would be a risk to bring him on."

This was neither the time nor the place for Thomas to explain how anxious he was to pay forward the grace that had been extended to him.

He also knew those who'd never had a troubled past couldn't understand the compulsion to help those who were working through their own troubles. Most youth in the church didn't spend their adolescence and young adult years having brushes with the law, as he had.

So he shrugged and prevaricated. "It just seemed like a *gut* match, putting someone interested in carpentry in contact with someone who owns a carpentry business. What better way to distract him from any further mischief?"

He vowed to say no more to Emma. Jeremy's situation mirrored his own misspent youth too closely. He didn't want her to guess just why he'd taken such a personal interest in the teen.

Emma had a feeling Thomas was dodging around something, but it was not the Amish way to pry. Still, a small shaft of concern lanced through her emotional gratitude for how he'd saved Hannah's life. Hyper-sensitive to clues that a future marriage might be just as disastrous as her past marriage, Emma decided to keep her thoughts regarding her change of heart about the possibility of courtship with Thomas to herself. It was better to approach the subject slowly anyway.

Yet at the same time she castigated herself for being overly cautious. No one was perfect. No man could be the perfect *hutband*. At least Thomas lacked the faults she had found insupportable in Hannah's father—the arrogance, the emotional battering, the verbal abuse. By contrast, Thomas was humble, quiet and eager to prove himself. Besides, Hannah adored him.

She looked at the child sitting in his lap drawing a picture on a blank sheet of paper with a pen. He would make a *gut* father.

But would he make a *gut hutband*?

And—something she hadn't really considered before—would she make a *gut* wife?

Self-analysis of this kind was foreign to her, but it was something to consider. Was she too emotionally scarred from her first marriage to be a helpmate and partner in a second marriage? She thought about her parents and their seemingly flawless union, and she wondered if she could ever rise to those kinds of standards.

"Speaking of thunderclouds," commented Thomas, "now it's your turn."

"Hmm?" She glanced up to see him watching her.

"You look like you have your own thunderstorm hovering overhead. Are you okay?"

She gave a tiny shake of her head. "*Ja*, fine. Just thinking, is all."

"Anything you can share?"

She thought for a moment. "*Nein.*" But she softened her refusal with a small smile.

Just then the doctor came in carrying a clipboard. He seemed delighted to see Thomas out of bed. "Good afternoon, Mr. Kemp. You look like you're feeling much better today."

Emma reached over to gently pull Hannah off his lap so he could talk to the doctor.

"I am," Thomas said, relinquishing the toddler. "I don't suppose it's possible to be discharged today?"

The doctor looked at the chart in his hands. "I'd rather hold you over one more night, but I'm confident you can leave tomorrow. Let me guess, you're still feeling very bruised and achy?"

"*Ja*, I am," Thomas admitted.

"And I think you'll find your stamina is quite a bit decreased," the doctor continued. "Right now, just out of bed, you probably feel like you can run a marathon. But you may feel differently once you start doing your normal activities. In a nutshell, don't overdo it."

"I'll try not to. I suppose I'm just feeling restless."

"That's a sign of improving health, believe it or not." The doctor looked at Emma. "And how are you and the baby feeling? Any ill effects from your tumble?"

"None for my daughter," she replied. "For me, it was just some soreness on the back of my head where I landed, and this bruise." She touched her cheek. She knew the discoloration was still visible but fading.

"Good. You're all three of you pretty tough cookies." The doctor made a note on the chart. "I'll see you in the morning, Mr. Kemp, and I'll sign off on your release." He smiled and left the room.

"Ah, freedom," sighed Thomas, leaning back in the chair. "It will be *gut* to get back to work."

"Only as much work as you're able," she retorted with a smile. "Doctor's orders. Don't overdo it."

"I have a feeling I couldn't overdo it even if I wanted. But I feel bad leaving the Yoders in a lurch so soon after they hired me."

"I've talked to Mabel. She hopes you'll take as long as needed to recuperate."

"*Ja*, true, but I still feel compelled to get back to work

as quickly as possible. I need to earn some money, if nothing else."

"Well, I think I can relieve your mind of one thing." Emma felt pleased to be the bearer of good news. "Quite a number of people in the church are interested in having you do the books for their businesses. I have a feeling you could open a store on Main Street and have plenty of clients besides the Yoders."

"Wow!" Thomas's whole face lit up. He leaned back in the chair, wincing a bit. "That's been one of the things I've most wanted to do since arriving—to have my own business. The Yoders would be my biggest clients, of course, but this way I can grow and expand beyond them."

"I think, if nothing else, your accident has given you a higher profile in the church. I know my uncle has been talking to a number of businesses within the church community that seem interested in having a part-time bookkeeper."

"Gott ist gut," he murmured. "I feel like I'm so far behind everyone else my age. I have no home, no transportation. But if I can keep my business growing, I'll be able to start obtaining those things for myself." He looked straight at her. "And maybe I'll earn enough to support a family."

"Maybe." Emma could feel her cheeks heat up. His meaning was clear. "But why are you so far behind, Thomas? You have all the usual skills of most men in the church, and some more besides. Not everyone has your ease with numbers or skills with accounting. What caused you to wait this long to buy a home or even a buggy?"

The same shutter she had seen before dropped over his expression. Whatever had happened in his past was locked behind it. She wondered if she would ever learn what he was hiding.

"I've had some extenuating circumstances," he replied blandly and said no more about the subject.

Emma gave a small inaudible sigh. She knew no one was perfect. No *hutband* could ever be perfect, either. She wondered if a courtship could proceed if such a significant part of his past would forever be sealed off from her.

She leaned back in the chair with Hannah cradled in her arms. Her daughter was getting sleepy. "So, let's say you get your bookkeeping business off the ground. Where do you see yourself in five years?"

He raised an eyebrow. "Do you really want to know?"

"*Ja*, sure, of course."

"Okay, but fair warning, I'll lay it on thick."

Now she was curious. "Okay, then."

He nodded. "I see myself baptized and a respectable member of the church," he began as if reciting a list he had memorized long ago. "I see my business thriving. I see myself as a happily married man with a wife who loves me and perhaps *kinner* to raise. I see myself living in a small house, something I can add to and expand to accommodate a growing family. I see myself with my own horse and buggy and a wagon. I see myself with a big garden and a pantry full of homegrown food. I see myself with some chickens and a cow I can milk. I see myself living happily ever after."

"Wow," breathed Emma. "You're right. That's pretty heavy stuff."

"Is it?" inquired Thomas. "I can achieve much of it myself through hard work and *Gott*'s help. Everything but the wife and *kinner*. I'll need help with that part."

The air was heavy with meaning. Emma hardly dared to breathe.

At her silence, an expression of concern crossed

Thomas's face. "Now," he said softly, "where do *you* see yourself in five years?"

She swallowed. "I thought we discussed that a few days ago. I saw myself as a single mother raising this little one to the best of my abilities."

"Is it really fair to raise her without a father?" he asked earnestly. "To deprive her of any siblings?"

Fear warred with desire inside her. A part of her still feared remarrying and making another mistake. Yet she longed for the happily-ever-after scenario Thomas had just painted. She had already decided she would welcome his courtship. So why was she suddenly getting cold feet?

"When d-did this conversation get so s-serious?" she stuttered.

"*Ja*, you're right." Some of the intensity seemed to drain out of him and he sat back in his chair with a rueful smile. "But funny things happen when one's life literally flashes before one's eyes. I could have died. But I didn't. *Gott* wanted me to live. And it seems I have a desire to live life to the fullest as a result."

And that life, she knew without a doubt, included her and Hannah. She touched Hannah's hair. The child had drifted off to sleep in her lap.

"Time will tell, Thomas," she said softly. "For now, I'm content to leave things in *Gott*'s hands."

Chapter Fifteen

Thomas was keyed up with anticipation to be released from the hospital, and by the time he had thanked the doctor and nurses for their care, Matthew Miller was waiting for him with his horse and buggy.

"Ah, it's *gut* to feel the fresh air." Thomas took a deep breath and released it.

"It's been quiet at the boardinghouse without you there," said Matthew, directing the horse to a side road that paralleled the main street to avoid traffic. "Not that you're there all day anyway, but it was strange having you gone."

"I'm anxious to get back to normal." Thomas nodded at a passerby who gave the buggy a small wave. "I'll go see the Yoders this afternoon and work out a schedule. The doctor said I shouldn't overdo it, but except for a little lingering soreness, I feel fine."

He'd felt fine until he'd set out for the Yoders. It was only a short walk, but by the time he climbed the porch steps in front of the mercantile, he had to pause and rest for a moment. His head swam. Okay, perhaps his optimism that he was fully recovered was a little misplaced. The doctor was right. He'd tired far more easily than he'd thought he would.

"Thomas!" Abe came around the counter as Thomas entered the door. He wrung Thomas's hand. "*Gut* to have you back. How are you feeling?"

Mabel came over to join the chorus of welcome. "It's nice to see you back on your feet."

He gave them what he trusted was a hearty smile. "I'm feeling better, but weaker than I'd hoped. It makes me glad bookkeeping requires a lot of sitting. I don't think I could swing a hammer right now."

Mabel made a clucking noise. "You're not to return to work until you're fully recovered, *ja*?"

He shook his head. "I don't know when 'fully recovered' might happen, but I'll be bored if I don't have something to do. Let me come in tomorrow for a couple hours and see how I do. The doctor told me it will take some time for my mind to unscramble, so I have no idea if I'll be able to concentrate for long."

Abe nodded. "Work at your own pace, Thomas. We're willing to be flexible."

"*Danke.*" Thomas felt a sudden pinprick of moisture in his eyes. The Yoders were truly good people.

He went back to the boardinghouse and slept most of the afternoon.

In the morning, dressed in fresh clothes, he made his way slowly back to the mercantile. He felt marginally better than yesterday and hoped he wouldn't have to leave too soon.

Mabel followed him into his office and dropped a hot scone and cup of coffee before him. When he began protesting, she silenced him with a smile. "Emma made arrangements to provide you with food for as long as you need it," she told him. "Now be quiet and enjoy it." She disappeared out the office door.

Thomas sipped his coffee. Emma had made arrangements to feed him, had she? He would have to thank her for that.

He pulled his ledgers and inventory sheets toward him and picked up where he'd left off before the accident.

While the numbers didn't jumble before his eyes as he'd feared, his mental stamina was definitely limited. A headache threatened at the back of his skull. He was just about to call it quits for the day when Mabel knocked lightly at his open office door. "Someone to see you, Thomas."

Thomas looked up and his jaw dropped. The visitor was Jeremy Watson.

The youth looked both sullen and remorseful. Thomas instinctively knew the boy had something important to say.

"*Danke*, Mabel," he said. "Would you mind closing the door on your way out?"

"*Ja*, sure." Mabel gave the boy a long look but left them alone.

In the sudden silence, Jeremy stared at the floor. Thomas kept his voice quiet. "Pull up a chair," he said.

Jeremy dropped into the visitor chair opposite the desk and clasped and unclasped his hands. "I'm sorry," he blurted.

"There's a lot behind those words," said Thomas. "What happened?"

As if a dam had burst, Jeremy's complete ugly story spilled out. "My parents… They never pay any attention to me. I thought taking the truck would make them notice me…"

At last, Thomas held up a hand to stop the bilge of information. Jeremy closed his mouth with a snap and resumed staring at his hands.

After letting the tension build up a moment or two, Thomas spoke and kept his voice gentle. "I'm sure you

know things could have been much, much worse," he
said. "I got battered and bruised, but if I'd still had the
baby in my arms, she could easily have been killed. I'd
say it was the hand of *Gott* that prevented that happening. In other words, my boy, you got very close to being
guilty of involuntary manslaughter."

"I know—"

Thomas silenced him again. "As I see it, this is your
great opportunity. You're standing at a fork in the road.
Down one path is a life of escalating crime that will eventually land you behind bars. Down the other path is a life
of respectability, hard work and success. It's up to you."

Jeremy stared at him for a moment. "Didn't you say
you were charged with involuntary manslaughter?"

"I was accused of it, yes. Thankfully, some video foot-
age showed I was nowhere near the scene when it happened, and my name was cleared. But that charge came
after ten years of thuggery on my part. I was a bad person, Jeremy, but taking someone's life—intentionally
or not—wasn't on my radar. Being accused of involuntary manslaughter was so terrifying that I saw my whole
future laid open in front of me. I begged for a second
chance, and I got it."

"Were you angry at your parents too?"

"*Nein*, not really. My parents were *gut* people. But
that's another sin on my soul. My parents were killed
in a buggy accident when I was about your age. It was
hard to admit that my behavior was at fault. I know my
father was distracted from my latest escapade and inattentively drove the buggy into traffic. It's not an easy
thing to be even indirectly responsible for the deaths of
one's own parents."

The boy's eyes widened and his mouth dropped open.

"A year ago, I was standing at the identical fork in

the road you're now facing," continued Thomas. "I was older, and my crimes were worse. By the hand of *Gott*, my brother offered me another chance. As a result, I have a bright future in front of me. I can't force you to do anything, but all I can tell you is I've been there and done that."

Jeremy twisted his hands. "What do I do?"

"Let me ask you something. When I stopped you from setting fire to the garbage cans in the park a while ago, you mentioned you might be interested in carpentry and construction. Is that true?"

"Yeah."

Thomas leaned back in his chair and ignored the threatening headache. "I know a man in our church who owns a log home construction company. He mentioned he's looking for an apprentice carpenter. When I suggested you might be interested and told him something about your background, he was too reluctant to take a risk on you. He says you're too big a liability."

The sullen look returned to the boy's face. "That's what everyone says. I never get a break."

"And who is responsible for that?"

"What do you mean?"

"I mean, who is responsible for the bad reputation you have?"

Jeremy sulkily picked at hole in his jeans. "Me, I guess," he muttered.

"And if Adam were to hire you and offer to teach you a trade, would you continue to be a troublemaker? Because if you so much as step a toe out of line, he'd fire you."

The teen looked up and, for the first time, Thomas saw a gleam of hope in the boy's eyes. "Do you think he'd really hire me?"

"I don't know. It might take some sweet-talking on

my part. I'll see him next after our church service on Sunday. I can lay your case before him again, but I can't guarantee anything."

A gleam of suspicion crossed the teen's face. "Why are you doing this for me?"

Thomas sighed. "Let me tell you another bit of my story. I didn't know how I was ever going to pay my brother back for the money he spent on an attorney to clear my name, but he didn't want me to pay him back. His exact words were, 'Pay it forward instead. Some-day, you're going to come across someone who needs help. Pay off your debt to me by helping them.'" Thomas paused. "Now do you understand why I'm interested in helping you?"

Jeremy had a bewildered expression on his face. Sud-denly, he looked very young and almost ready to weep. "S-so I'm the one you want to pay it forward to?"

"If you're interested in taking the gift, *ja*."

The boy blinked hard a few times. "Is that what you're calling it, a gift?"

"What else would you call it? I was given a gift, Jer-emy. It changed my life. My hope is you'll accept this gift too."

The teen's mouth worked but no sound came out.

Thomas knew better than to push. Instead, he waved the boy out of his office with a small smile. "Go on, now. You have a lot to think over. We can talk about it later."

Without a word, Jeremy stumbled to his feet, stag-gered to the office door and let himself out.

Thomas prayed his gift would be accepted.

Emma kissed Hannah goodbye, left the child with her Aunt Lois and walked to another church member's home to do some housecleaning. She had several elderly women who appreciated the deep-cleaning efforts a younger woman could do, and Emma was always happy to supplement her income. Today's client was Esther Mast, a widow whose daughter was, rather surprisingly, an Amish veterinarian in town.

Emma hummed a hymn under her breath as she pulled the wagon, this time filled with cleaning tools and supplies, along the road. She tried not to think about Thomas and her confused feelings for him. Instead, she let the sunshine wash across her and listened to the sounds of the crickets and birds. A bald eagle flew overhead, and she tracked it with her eyes.

The gravel roads of the settlement seldom saw any vehicles except horse-drawn buggies, wagons and the occasional bicycle. Nor did any townspeople venture very often into the midst of the church community. So when Emma saw a young man ahead of her dressed in *Englisch* clothes, she actually drew up short and stared. Who was he, and what was he doing here?

He appeared very young, no more than a teenager, and was dressed in blue jeans and a T-shirt. He walked with purpose, as if heading for a specific destination. Since Emma was heading in the same general direction, she found herself following a few hundred feet behind him.

The fenced-in construction yard of Adam Chupp loomed ahead. The compound had a wide gate facing the road. The teenager stopped in front of the gate, hesitated a few moments and then went into the compound. Emma saw him approach one of the workmen, who pointed toward the small structure Adam used as an office. The teen nodded and made for the office. He entered and disappeared inside.

Now what was that all about? Emma continued walking toward Esther Mast's home, pondering the incident.

She had a nagging feeling there was more to the seemingly trivial event than met the eye. She wondered if the teen was Jeremy, the boy Thomas wanted to help.

Throughout the afternoon as she scrubbed floors and washed windows at Esther's small cottage, she thought about the incident. It made her wonder anew why helping the teen was so important to Thomas. She had an uneasy feeling there was a fairly serious reason, but he was reluctant to tell her. She wondered if it was tied into his refusal to go into his past.

His past. His mysterious past. That was probably the single biggest fly in her ointment. As interesting and attractive as Thomas was, Emma wasn't willing to trade her independence for another marriage until all cards were laid on the table. That included a full confession of what motivated Thomas—the good, the bad and the ugly. Only then could she make a decision about whether she would welcome his courtship.

She finished her business at Esther's, accepted her payment, and started back toward her aunt and uncle's home to collect Hannah. She peered hard at Adam Chupp's log yard as she passed but saw no further glimpse of the *Englisch* teenager.

Returning to her aunt and uncle's home, she saw Hannah working with Aunt Lois in the garden in front of the house. Hannah saw her from afar, tossed down her little trowel and started running to meet her. It was inevitable the child would trip and fall on the way, and a wail soon cut over the cheerful sound of birdsong.

"*Liebling*, you should know better than to run on gravel," crooned Emma as she picked up the toddler and soothed her. Hoisting the child onto her hip, she took the wagon handle with her other hand and finished the trek to the garden.

"How did the housecleaning go?" inquired Lois. The older woman straightened up and arched her back, stretching out the muscles.

"Fine. Esther says hello." Emma put Hannah down and distracted the child from her fall with a question. "What were you and Aunt Lois working on? Can you show me?"

Hannah sniffed away her tears and toddled over to pick some carrots. "Can we have some for dinner?"

"Leave those with Aunt Lois," suggested Emma. "We have plenty of carrots of our own. Is your back hurting again?" she asked her aunt.

"*Ja*. It's getting harder to bend over a hoe." The older woman gave a sigh of frustration. "I don't know how much longer I'll be able to keep gardening."

"Well, I can easily garden enough for both you and Uncle Samuel," Emma offered. "Do you want me to clean the house for you this week?"

"I wouldn't mind it," Lois admitted. She picked up the basket of carrots and waded through the tidy garden rows toward the porch. "How's Thomas doing?"

"Fine. Here, I'll take that." Emma took the basket from her aunt and added, "I saw him yesterday. He's able to work for a couple hours at a time now."

"That's *gut*. Also, your uncle had an idea. See that shed over there?"

Emma followed Lois's pointing finger toward a spacious barn-style shed perched on the edge of their property. It was halfway between their house and Emma's own small cabin. "*Ja?*"

"Thomas expressed an interest in having his own office for a bookkeeping business. Your uncle thought the shed might work as a stand-alone office, if it's retrofitted correctly. That way, he'll be more central to everyone out here in the settlement."

"Except for the Yoders." Emma regarded the shed with interest. "Right now, there's only a block and a half between where he's living and where he's working."

"*Ja*, but he's not going to want to live in the boardinghouse forever."

Emma shot her aunt a look, but the older woman's face was guileless. "If he's not living in the boardinghouse, where else would he live?"

"Oh, I'm sure some place can be found for him out here in the settlement. Soon he'll be in a position to get on with his life. You know—home, wife, *kinner*, that kind of thing."

"Auntie, I don't think you can plan out Thomas's life for him."

"Or you either, *ja*?"

"*Ja*. Or me either. I know what you're thinking, Aunt Lois, but these things can't be hurried."

"Just don't dangle him along."

"Believe me, I'm not dangling Thomas along. Besides, even if we decided to court, we'd have a long ways to go, especially since he still has to get baptized." Her good humor restored, Emma smiled at her aunt. "Don't rush your fences, Aunt Lois. And I promise not to rush mine. Besides…" She gestured toward Hannah, for whom the conversation thankfully was not truly comprehensible. "I have this one to think about. She's my biggest priority right now."

Aunt Lois raised her eyebrows. "If you're looking at that as an excuse to delay, it won't work. I don't think I've ever seen a child choose her own father before, but it sure strikes me that this little one has already done so."

Emma stopped dead in her tracks, momentarily poleaxed.

Nuts. Her aunt was right.

Chapter Sixteen

"A shed, eh?" Thomas took a bite of macaroni salad and chewed thoughtfully.

It was good to be back at a church service. While sitting with the bishop during the meal afterward, the older man had brought up the possibility of converting the shed into an office space.

"*Ja*, it's about ten by fifteen feet," explained the bishop. "It's right on the edge of our property. It will need some work, but it's close to the road and in a convenient location, assuming most of your future clientele are church members."

"But there's a problem," said Thomas. "I'm mostly working for the Yoders right now. While they're supportive of the idea of me going freelance and keeping them as clients, I'm only living a block and a half away from the store." Thomas took another forkful of food. "It would probably make more sense to lease an office in town when that time comes. Or perhaps the Yoders will rent me the room I'm currently using in the store itself."

"*Ja*, I can see those concerns." The bishop bit into a chicken wing and spoke with his mouth full. "But the offer stands. If you ever want to use that shed, let me know."

"Danke." Thomas wondered at the offer. Not that it wasn't a welcome option—having options was a good thing—but he was nowhere near ready to launch his own business. Not when he was still dealing with the physical aftermath of his accident.

He remembered the shed, having passed it a number of times. It occurred to him that the shed, located at the edge of the bishop's property, was only a short distance from Emma's adjoining land. Thomas wondered if the offer was solely altruistic, or if Samuel had something else up his sleeve.

Adam Chupp, carrying a plateful of food, joined Thomas and the bishop. After a brief prayer over the meal, Adam said without preamble, "Thomas, I owe you an apology."

"For what?" Thomas was bewildered.

"For doubting you. I think Jeremy Watson will turn into a fine worker after all."

"You met him?" His jaw dropped.

"You didn't send him?" Adam looked surprised.

Thomas was bewildered. "Send him where? What are you talking about?"

"Hmm." Adam broke open a biscuit and buttered it. "Maybe you don't know." He smiled. "Jeremy walked into my office in the log yard about a week ago. He introduced himself, said he heard from you that I was looking for an apprentice carpenter, and he'd like to be considered."

"You're kidding!" Thomas's eyes widened. "That took guts."

"So you didn't put him up to it?"

"Nein. Not at all. Did he, ah, tell you about his transgressions?"

"Ja, all of them. Or what I assume is all of them. He certainly didn't hold back, but he said he's eager to

change his ways and learn a trade. Something about turning over a new leaf."

Thomas was floored. So the boy had taken his advice to heart after all. He closed his eyes, pinched the bridge of his nose and murmured, *"Gott ist gut."* Then out loud, he said, "He came into my office at the Yoder's to apologize for the accident. I mentioned our previous conversation, Adam, about having him apprentice with you, and how you had legitimate concerns for his delinquent history. I told him he was standing at a crossroad, and he could either go down a *gut* path in life or a bad path. Then I sent him on his way to think things over. I certainly didn't recommend he go talk with you."

Adam looked grudgingly impressed. "So he took it upon himself. That's *gut*." He took a bite of food and swallowed it before continuing. "If he wants to truly turn over a new leaf, time will tell."

"So you've changed your mind? You're willing to take a chance on him?" Thomas hoped his voice didn't sound too eager.

"Ja. He's going to start working after school and on Saturdays as needed. I told him I'd give him a trial period to see how he works out. He'll need training, but that's okay. That's what I expected with an apprentice anyway."

Thomas suddenly felt like weeping, but he repressed the emotion. His overwhelming thought was that he was at last paying forward the grace his brother had extended to him. Blinking hard, he stared at his plate. *"Danke*, Adam. *Vielen dank.* This means a lot to me, and I hope it works out."

"Well, it's not all charity on my part." Adam appeared unaware of Thomas's surge of emotion. "I'll work the kid hard. My business is booming, and he might be just one of several kids I'll hire. But if he works out, he's got a job as long as I'm in business."

A woman's voice called out and Adam jerked around. "Looks like Ruth is ready to go. *Faeriwell*, gentlemen." Adam collected his plate and rose from the picnic table.

The bishop had remained silent through the exchange between Adam and Thomas. Now by themselves, the older man raised compassionate eyes. *"Gott* ist *gut,"* he affirmed.

Since Bishop Beiler knew the true reason behind Thomas's interest in the teen, Thomas nodded. "I had no idea Jeremy took the initiative to go see Adam on his own. Adam is right. It does sound like the boy's looking to change. Samuel, I see so much of myself in that *youngie* it's almost frightening."

"Don't dismiss your own journey, Thomas." Samuel sipped some lemonade. "If your past life was as bad as you say, you've made a remarkable turnaround."

"It's all *Gott*'s doing. I can't tell you how much I'm looking forward to being baptized and a full church member."

"I look forward to it too. Lots of people do, including my niece."

Thomas shot the older man a look. "Meaning...?"

"Meaning if I should someday have a man like you in the family, I would be very happy."

Thomas's emotions warred between pleasure and annoyance. Blatant matchmaking wasn't common within the church, but this was coming from the bishop.

"It's a little soon to think along those lines," he said cautiously. It didn't matter that his own thoughts were firmly along those lines. His romantic life was none of the bishop's business.

"Ja, sure, I understand that. But let me put it this way—it would not be an unwelcome development."

"*Danke.* I think," Thomas joked awkwardly.

"Besides," continued the bishop in a quiet voice, "your background may actually benefit our new settlement."

Thomas was startled. "How?" he croaked. "My background is horrible."

"Precisely. But your background allowed you to understand and counsel the *Englisch* boy, ain't so? Your experience on the darker side of life might be useful if some other *youngies* within our church community ever start to go wrong."

"But it's my hope that my background will never be known," argued Thomas, keeping his voice low. He didn't want anyone overhearing. He was a little alarmed at the thought of his secret getting out.

"Well, no one will hear it from me," Samuel assured him. "Nonetheless, you bring a unique perspective to our church community. You'll be in an exceptional position to counsel others who might go astray. I don't know if you realize how much I admire your turnaround, Thomas. Not many people could bring themselves back from the brink and make the decision to become an upstanding and respectable member of the church. It was hard, but you did it."

For the second time in fifteen minutes, Thomas had to blink back moisture. Praise from such an esteemed person as the bishop was praise indeed.

"*Danke,*" he murmured.

A silence fell between the two men for a few moments. Thomas's thoughts were in a whirl. If he wanted acceptance, it seemed he had found it here in Montana. His future—so bleak only a year ago—sparkled with the promise of so many blessings…

"And you've fulfilled your goal," continued the bishop, as if he, too, had been following an internal train of thought. "If this situation with Jeremy and Adam works out, you've paid your debt to your brother. Does that bring you satisfaction?"

"Ja," replied Thomas, pulling his thoughts back to the conversation. "When I was talking to Jeremy in my office the other day, I wondered just how much my advice would sink in. *Youngies* don't always want to be corrected by adults. At least, I never did. My life would certainly have turned out differently if I'd been able to *hear* what people were trying to tell me. I had to be 'scared straight,' as the saying goes. I think Jeremy's accident with the pickup truck did the same thing."

"Gott works in mysterious ways," agreed the bishop. "It still gives me nightmares how much worse it could have been." His eyes focused on little Hannah playing in a sandbox with some other small children. "I love my little grandniece to pieces. Lois and I would have been devastated if something had happened to her—to say nothing of Emma. We are eternally in your debt, Thomas, if for no other reason than you saved her life."

"I'm not used to being the recipient of gratitude," said Thomas in a low voice. "I've spent my life cultivating anger and sowing dissent. This is a new feeling for me."

"And hopefully a lasting one. But enough solemnity. I have a hankering to try one of Esther Mast's blueberry-cheesecake tarts. If you've never had one, you're in for a treat." The older man rose and indicated Thomas should follow him to the tables where the food was spread out.

Thomas rose as well. He had entered the community as a supplicant desperate to make a good name for himself. And now, in just a few short weeks, he had succeeded.

Gott was indeed *gut*.

* * *

On Monday morning, Emma loaded Hannah into the wagon along with a large basket of cleaning supplies—scrub brush, window squeegee, rags, cleaning solutions—and walked to her aunt and uncle's home to do some housecleaning for her aunt.

"What do you want to do with Aunt Lois while I'm busy?" she asked the child.

Hannah was silent a moment. "Garden?" she finally said.

Emma chuckled. "You're a daughter after my own heart. *Ja*, ask Aunt Lois if you can do something in the garden. Just remember, her back hurts her. That's why I'm cleaning the house, after all."

"*Ja, Mamm*. Look! Robin!" Hannah pointed.

"*Ja*, and look there. It's a meadowlark."

Emma continued her usual identification game as they trundled down the gravel road the quarter mile to the Beiler house.

On the way, they passed the large shed Aunt Lois had suggested might work as an office for Thomas. She was right. It would be ideal—more so *if* she and Thomas were married.

At her aunt and uncle's, she lifted Hannah out of the wagon and reached for the basket of cleaning tools. The child dashed up on the porch, banged once or twice on the door and managed to twist the knob to go inside. Emma smiled at her daughter's enthusiasm. It was true, Hannah didn't have a father. It was also true that Emma's parents were too far away in Indiana to be a meaningful part of her life. But right here, practically next door, were surrogate grandparents who were just as wonderful and added a richness to the little girl's life.

"Guder mariye," she called, stepping inside the door Hannah had left open.

"Guder mariye," Aunt Lois replied. Emma saw the child had already climbed into Lois's lap and was chattering about the garden.

"How's your back this morning?" Emma lifted the basket of cleaning supplies onto the kitchen table.

"Better," her aunt replied. "I think I just tweaked it last week. But I know from experience I need to keep resting it, so I'm grateful you can do some housecleaning for me today."

"Should Hannah be sitting in your lap?"

"Ja, that's no trouble. Now lifting her up—that's what I shouldn't be doing."

"Do you hear that, *liebling*?" Emma addressed her daughter. "Aunt Lois can't pick you up, so don't ask, okay?"

"Ja, Mamm."

"Is Uncle Samuel home?" inquired Emma.

"Nein, he went to visit the Kings. He'll be back around noon. It would be a *gut* time to clean his office, since he seldom lets me in there when he's working." Lois chuckled.

"I'd best get busy, then."

Emma's preferred method of housecleaning was to go from one end of a home to the other. She started with her aunt and uncle's bedroom, where she made up the bed with fresh sheets, dusted the furniture and swept the floor.

It gave her pleasure to help the older couple, who had been so good to her. Emma's frame of mind improved as she worked her way through the house, leaving it sparkling in her wake. Through the window, she saw Lois sitting on a bench in the garden while watching Hannah. The child was picking small bits of leaves and bringing them to Lois, doubtless herbs. Emma smiled at the tab-leau and continued with her tasks.

Entering the kitchen, she wondered if she should make lunch. She walked toward the front door and called into the garden, "Aunt Lois, should I make lunch before Uncle Samuel returns?"

"*Nein*, don't bother," her aunt called back. "He usually just likes a sandwich for lunch."

"*Ja, gut.*" Emma returned to the kitchen, washed the breakfast dishes, wiped the counters and swept the floor.

The last room to clean was her uncle's office. Emma had seldom been in this room where her uncle managed church-related business. It was outfitted simply with two filing cabinets, a plain oak desk and chair, and two visitor chairs. A spacious basket on the desk held Uncle Samuel's beautiful calico cat, Thomasina. The animal lifted its head from a nap, blinked sleepily and, almost imme-diately, an outsized purr filled the room.

"Hello, you beautiful thing." Emma spent a moment or two scratching the cat under the chin. She knew the animal had been attacked by a coyote a couple years ear-lier and had nearly died. As a result, Uncle Samuel was fonder of the animal than ever before.

Leaving the cat to continue her nap, Emma dusted off the windowsills, file cabinets and chairs. Then she turned her attention to her uncle's desk, strewn as always with files and papers. She didn't try to organize anything, since she knew it wasn't her business to do so. But she dusted the edges and corners of the desk and then picked up her broom and prepared to sweep the office floor.

Something on the desk caught her gaze and she peered closer—first with curiosity and then with interest.

It was a manila file with a tab labeled Kemp, Thomas.

The file was closed, but the papers within were partially fanned out.

A multipage typewritten letter lay partly exposed, with the intriguing heading My Past. Glancing guiltily toward the office door—the house was quiet, since Aunt Lois was still outside with Hannah—Emma withdrew the letter and began to read. Her eyes widened.

The letter was long, with several sheets stapled together. It was clearly a testimonial from Thomas detailing his past, evidently as a full confession before being accepted as a candidate to move to the Montana settlement. And what a letter it was.

Emma nearly choked on bile as she read his litany of transgressions going back years. Petty theft, thuggery, bullying, even the indirect cause of death of his own parents—the letter went from bad to worse.

Then the term "involuntary manslaughter" leaped out at her. Involuntary manslaughter! Before she could read further, she heard the unmistakable sounds of a horse and buggy as her uncle returned from his errand.

Emma dropped the letter and leaped back from the desk. The broom she had been balancing in the crook of her arm clattered to the floor, causing the cat to jerk its head up and stare at her with startled eyes.

As the sound of her uncle's voice speaking to Aunt Lois got closer, she shoved the letter back in the file, trying to recapture the position it was in before she had peeked at it. Then she grabbed the broom and her dust cloths and beat a hasty retreat from the office, taking fast refuge in the kitchen.

She was breathing hard, as if she had been running. She pressed a hand to her chest, gulping. *This?* This was the man her aunt and uncle were pushing on her as a possible match? A man with a criminal past? A man guilty of involuntary manslaughter? Her blood ran cold at the thought of such a man being close to her child. It ran even colder at the thought of her marrying him. By the grace of *Gott*, she had escaped one insupportable marriage. Was seeing that letter *Gott*'s way of letting her escape a possible second mistake?

She had to get hold of herself before her uncle saw her distress and asked her what was wrong. Thinking fast, she yanked a bottle of ammonia from her basket of cleaning supplies and poured some on the table. She made a show of choking and coughing as she wiped it up just as her uncle walked in.

He saw her and stopped. "Are you okay?"

"*Ja.* Sorry," she gasped, knowing her cheeks and her eyes were red. "I spilled some ammonia."

"*Ach*, do you need help?" He coughed once or twice himself as the fumes rose.

"*Nein.* But keep Hannah out, *bitte.* I don't want her smelling this."

Her uncle retreated.

Emma would have given a sigh of relief but the ammonia fumes made that impossible. Instead, she made sure the kitchen window was open, repacked her basket and headed outside. There, she gulped the fresh air, glad for an excuse for her agitation.

"*Mamm* okay?" asked Hannah.

"*Ja*, I'm okay, *liebling.* Just breathed in something nasty." Emma fished a handkerchief from her pocket and mopped her face.

"The house is clean," she told her aunt. "I'm so sorry about spilling the ammonia. It should be okay to go into the kitchen within a couple minutes."

"*Ach, vielen dank* for doing this for me, *lieb*," said her aunt.

Emma swung Hannah onto her hip. "I'd best be going. Hannah and I are going to can some carrots this afternoon, aren't we, little one?" She had to get away from her aunt and uncle as fast as possible.

After saying her goodbyes, she placed Hannah into the wagon, loaded in the basket and set off down the road.

She had a lot of thinking to do. A lot of hard, bitter thinking.

Chapter Seventeen

By the end of the week, Thomas was more or less back to normal after the accident. His mind was clearer, and he was able to work a full day at his books, though he had to admit to being profoundly fatigued by each evening. His body was still a bit achy, but nothing he couldn't handle.

October had dawned over the town and Thomas found he liked autumn in the mountains. The air smelled crisp and sweet and faintly of apples from a profusion of wild fruit trees growing in fields and along roadsides. The town's farmer's market was in full swing each Saturday in the park, and he enjoyed browsing the booths, quite a few of which were run by fellow church members selling surplus garden produce.

Standing at the edge of the park and watching the bustling crowds, Thomas had a moment of profound gratitude to *Gott*. A year ago, his future was bleak. Today, his future was bright. He had helped Jeremy Watson straighten himself out. And—he prayed—he might have a future with Emma and Hannah.

He hadn't seen Emma or her daughter since the last Sabbath service, and he wondered why. She hadn't been working in the store, and he missed her. He missed Hannah too. Glancing at the sun, he decided to ride his bike out to see them.

First, he purchased some fresh ginger at one of the booths at the farmer's market, since he knew it was a spice she didn't grow. Then he went back to the boarding-house, strapped the bag of ginger onto the bicycle's rack and took off for the three-mile ride to the church settlement. He sucked in great lungful of the clear, pure air as he pedaled. It felt good to be exercising again.

As he anticipated, Emma was working in her garden with little Hannah at her side as he rode up. His heart swelled with love at the sight of them.

"Hi! Hi!" Hannah squealed when she saw him, dropped whatever she had been doing and ran toward the fence.

Emma straightened and shaded her eyes as he approached, but she had no smile of welcome. Looking at her face, he felt a foreboding shiver make its way through him before he quickly dismissed it. It was fall. Gardens needed a lot of attention before the first frost. Undoubtedly, she had just been overwhelmed with work and hadn't been able to make it into town.

He glided to a stop, dismounted and wheeled the bicycle around the garden's perimeter as Hannah trotted along inside the fence. When she reached the gate, she launched herself out and into his arms.

He chuckled and scooped up the child. "*Guder nammi-daag, liebling.* Are you being a *gut* girl for your *mamm*?"

"*Ja!* We're picking beans. Look." The child pointed toward the bean patch.

Emma was still bent over her task and hadn't greeted him. The foreboding returned, curling like acid in Thomas's midsection.

"I brought something for your *mamm*," he said, using

one hand to unstrap the bag of ginger and hand it to the child. "It's ginger."

He put Hannah down and the child darted into the garden with the bag in her hands. "*Mamm*, look! Ginger."

"*Ja, gut.* Would you mind putting this in the kitchen, *liebling*?" Emma addressed the child but did not look at him. Hannah darted off.

Thomas waded among the plants, searching for a welcome from the woman he had come to love and finding nothing.

"*Guder nammidaag*, Emma," he said. "I've missed you this week."

"*Guder nammidaag,*" she replied, her hands busy as she plucked green beans. "*Ja*, it's been a busy week."

"What's the matter?"

"Nothing."

He felt a moment's annoyance at the blatant lie. "Of course something's the matter. You're doing your best to pretend I'm not even here. Why?"

She straightened and he nearly staggered back at the pain and anger in her eyes. "If you want to know the truth," she snapped, "it's that I don't feel like associating with a man who committed involuntary manslaughter."

He paled and did stagger back a step or two now. By some means, she had clearly found out about his past—or thought she had.

"I never committed involuntary manslaughter," he said. "Whoever told you that is wrong."

"You said so in your own words!"

Now he was baffled. "Emma, what are you talking about? What words?"

"In your letter to my uncle."

Understanding dawned. She had clearly seen the full confession he had written to the bishop before migrating to Montana. But—had she read the *whole thing*? It didn't sound as if she had.

"You're under a huge misunderstanding," he assured her. "I was cleared of all charges."

"It's not just that." He saw tears in her eyes. "There's so much about you I don't know. I—I can't trust you. You're a liar, Thomas, and I won't allow myself to be courted by a liar."

Anger rose inside him and he kept a tight rein on it. "I'm not a liar," he replied in a controlled voice. "I simply omitted things I was ashamed of. Why do you think I came out here to Montana? Why do you think I wanted a new start and to put my past behind me? I'm a new man, Emma, and don't you ever doubt that."

"How can I help but doubt?" She bent over the beans once more, taking a fast swipe across her eyes as she did so.

Looking at her industrious hands and shuttered face, Thomas despaired of being able to penetrate the barriers she had erected around herself. "So, you're going to act as judge, jury and executioner," he said in a weary voice, "without allowing me to speak in my own defense."

"What is there to defend?" She dropped some picked beans into the basket at her feet. "I read what you did when you were a *youngie*. I can't have my child exposed to that kind of behavior."

"Behavior stemming from when I was a *youngie*? Is that fair, Emma?" He tried to keep his temper in check but anger bled through.

She straightened and met his gaze. "Fair or not, it frightens me that I nearly gave my heart to someone who so closely resembles my first husband in disposition. Leave me alone, Thomas. I have work to do." She picked up her basket and moved to another section of beans, her back toward him in a gesture of dismissal.

Red-hot fury lanced through him at her behavior. He stood rooted for a moment, his fists clenched, as he fought the unworthy emotion. The Amish did not approve of raw anger. It led to crimes of passion and he had spent too much of his life letting anger rule him and his actions.

If he was the new man he'd told Emma he was, anger could have no part of him. He closed his eyes, said a prayer for control and took some deep breaths. He opened his eyes and looked at her industrious figure laboring over the vegetables. "This isn't over, Emma," he said quietly. "Whatever you've built up in your mind against me isn't true. I'm nothing like your first husband, and I will prove it." He spun on his heel and marched out of the garden.

"Mr. Thomas! Mr. Thomas!" wailed Hannah from the porch steps.

He didn't dare stop to comfort the child, not with her mother so immobile on the issue. Thomas mounted the bicycle and pedaled to escape the toddler's wails of frustration.

Was it just half an hour ago that he'd been feeling so optimistic about his future? Now, not so much.

He wondered how Emma could have misinterpreted his written confessional so badly. In the letter, he had made it crystal clear to the bishop that he was nowhere near the scene of the crime and had been fully exonerated in court. He'd also confessed the pain and shame of his past crimes and his fervent desire to put that life behind him.

And he had. Until this point, he'd been astounded at the sweetness and promise of a life well lived, at the contrast between the transgressions of his younger days and the potential life of respectability that lay ahead of him.

But if Emma remained immobile, he didn't know if he had a future here in Montana after all. Maybe he should return to Indiana. He knew his brother would give him his old job back in a heartbeat. He tried to pump his legs on the bicycle pedals, translating his anger into speed as he glared at the gravel road before him, but had to slow down since his body was still recovering.

Through his hurt and anger, he had a thread of understanding for Emma's changed attitude.

The pain she still felt about her first husband clearly lingered. She was scared of making another marital mistake. He understood that. How could he convince her he was nothing like the man he'd been even a year ago? How could he convince her he was a risk worth taking? How? How?

A year ago, he would not have understood the concept of fighting for what he wanted. Now he did. Emma and Hannah were worth fighting for. He wouldn't turn tail and slink back to Indiana. No, he was going to stay here in Montana, in the new life of promise he was building, and fight for the woman and child he had come to love.

Somehow, he had to pierce that hard shell she had built around her heart. His whole future depended on it.

"Mr. Thomas! Mr. Thomas!" Hannah cried at the retreating bicycle. She dissolved into tears.

Emma's heart, hardened as it was against the man she'd started to love, melted over the child she adored. "There, there, *liebling*," she crooned, scooping the child up in her arms. "Mr. Thomas just had to leave, that's all."

"Didn't say bye-bye." The toddler buried her face in Emma's shoulder and wept, inconsolable.

Carrying her, Emma sat down on a porch rocking chair and rocked the child. Was Thomas so important to Hannah's happiness? Emma's surety that she could raise her daughter without a husband hadn't changed. She was perfectly capable of doing so, and Hannah had all kinds of father figures within the church community to provide the vital male balance.

But was it enough?

Emma remembered her own father's quiet strength and day-to-day presence while growing up. As good men do, he guided his sons and daughters to walk upright within their family, their faith and their community. Emma wished, not for the first time, she had chosen to wait for a man with similar characteristics.

Emma leaned her head back in the rocker and closed her eyes. Prayers wouldn't even come. Instead, despair crept into her soul. Was she doing her daughter wrong?

For a few glorious weeks, she had thought her future had promise. Thomas had seemed like everything her first husband was not. He was quiet, he was strong, he worked hard and he had saved Hannah's life. For her part, Hannah adored him. She had from the start.

From the start… Emma opened her eyes and stared blindly at the garden basking in the mid-October sunshine. Literally from the first moment she'd met him, Hannah had shown a curious affinity for Thomas, glomming onto him at every opportunity. He had returned the child's affection.

Some people said young children were closer to *Gott* because they didn't yet have any of the social norms, biases and other distractions people imposed on each other. Was Hannah showing her own mother *Gott*'s will that Thomas was the right person to marry?

And yet…involuntary manslaughter, on top of a life-time of thuggery. Emma shuddered.

Ever since seeing that letter in her uncle's office, Emma had stewed over Thomas's background. Unable and unwilling to discuss it with anyone, the issue had grown in her mind. It had swelled and blown up until Thomas's past was as large and looming as a volcano. Somehow, it had become mixed with the verbal and emotional abuse she had suffered at the hands of her first husband until she was actually confusing the two men.

As difficult as Simeon had been, he hadn't committed the long list of crimes Thomas had confessed to in that letter. Sure, Thomas talked a good game now, but what might happen after vows were said? People changed after they got married, Emma knew that. Most changed for the good, but some changed for the bad. Simeon had changed for the bad, and if *Gott* hadn't taken him when He had, Emma would still be yoked with someone who not only treated his wife with contempt, but might treat his own child badly. After all, Simeon hadn't wanted a baby, at least not at that point in his life. The term he'd used was *shackled*.

For the first time in a long time, Emma wondered if Simeon had felt even more trapped than she had in a loveless marriage with a baby on the way. Was that why he had taken out his frustration on her? Would it have escalated into physical abuse?

Well, that was behind her now. *Gott* had taken Simeon and freed Emma from the *shackles* of a bad marriage.

Hannah cried herself to sleep. Rocking her on the porch, Emma felt overwhelming love for her daughter, a mama bear's fierce desire to protect her from life's up-heavals and tragedies. She knew that wish was unreason-able. No parent could protect a child from everything.

She gave a small rueful snort. She was proof of that. She well remembered the dismay and disappointment of her own parents when she'd confessed she was pregnant out of wedlock. It didn't matter that Simeon was not someone she would have chosen as a lifelong partner. She'd had to marry him because of the poor timing of the beloved child she now held in her arms.

Well, *Gott* in His infinite wisdom had seen fit to release her from the chains of matrimony to a man she didn't love, just as He had seen fit to bless her with the most wonderful child anyone could hope for.

But where did Thomas fit into all this?

Emma frowned. In her righteous anger over discovering just how bad his past behavior had been, was she overlooking his *present* behavior? She had to admit, until she'd read that letter, she'd had nothing but praise for his behavior, conduct, attitude and work ethic.

She gulped, suddenly near tears. She was so confused. She was petrified of making a similar mistake to the one she had made before. Yet part of her longed for a solid, happy marriage, something like the one her parents had. Or Aunt Lois and Uncle Samuel.

Until she'd met Thomas, she hadn't even considered the possibility of remarrying. He was the only one who had shaken her conviction to stay single.

But…*involuntary manslaughter*? Years of thuggery and mayhem? That was a lot to overlook. On paper, Thomas looked like a bad risk. Could she subject Hannah's future—and her own—to a man who might "flip" back to how he behaved before?

Her mind went back and forth, bringing her no closer to finding a solution than when she'd first seen that letter.

She couldn't sort through this herself. She had to talk to somebody. The most logical people were her aunt and uncle—not least because they were apparently the only ones fully aware of Thomas's background.

She heaved a sigh. No time like the present.

She hated to disturb the slumbering child, but Emma knew she wouldn't be able to rest until she had more insight into the situation. Moving gently, she stood up and carefully hitched Hannah higher onto her shoulder. She walked down the porch steps, laid the child on the cushions in the wagon, and started on the quarter-mile walk to her aunt and uncle's house.

Within ten minutes, she was in her aunt and uncle's yard.

Aunt Lois was sitting in a rocking chair on the porch, a bowl of green beans in her lap, trimming the ends. She looked up at Emma's approach, but her smile of greeting was wiped off her face. "Emma! Is everything okay?"

At the sound of the words, Hannah moved and lifted her sleepy head. "*Mamm*? *Was ist es?*"

"Shh. I just decided to visit Aunt Lois and Uncle Samuel, *liebling*. Do you want to see Aunt Lois?"

"*Ja...*" The toddler dropped her head back to the cushions and rubbed her eyes.

Emma lifted the child from the wagon and walked up to the porch. "I needed to talk to you and Uncle Samuel," she told her aunt.

"Here, I'll take her." Lois put the bowl of beans aside and reached for the toddler. Emma transferred her daughter into the older woman's motherly arms, and Lois started rocking with the child in her lap.

"Where's Uncle Samuel?" Emma knew her voice sounded strangled.

"In his office." Lois shot her a look. "Do you want me to hold Hannah while you go talk to him?"

Gratitude for the older woman's insight and discretion washed over Emma. *"Ja, bitte."*

"Go on, then. Hannah and I are fine." Lois dropped a kiss on the top of the toddler's head.

Emma went into the house. Then she paused a moment and pressed a hand to her chest, praying for guidance. She had a feeling this discussion with her uncle—both as her closest relative as well as the settlement's bishop—could make or break her future.

Samuel Beiler was a wise man. His job was to watch over the spiritual welfare of his church. He would not have willingly taken a criminal into the Montana settlement. Why had he accepted Thomas? What did her uncle know that she didn't?

She knew it was wrong to pry into her uncle's paperwork, but she was glad she had. It had opened her eyes to an issue she hadn't known existed, and that must—absolutely must—be cleared up before she would allow herself to engage her emotions further. In fact, it annoyed her that her uncle had seen fit to keep Thomas's background a secret, especially while encouraging a courtship between them. Why would he do such a thing?

One thing was clear. She had to know why her uncle had accepted a man like Thomas into the Montana settlement if his background was as bad as it sounded from the letter. There had to be a reason.

Chapter Eighteen

Emma saw her uncle sitting at his desk, writing something. She rapped on the doorframe.

He looked up. "Emma! *Guder nammidaag...*" His voice trailed when he saw her expression. His smile of greeting was wiped off his face in a manner comically similar to his wife's. "Is something wrong?"

"*Ja.* Badly. I need to talk to you, Uncle Samuel."

"Of course." He gestured toward a chair.

Emma seated herself and clasped and unclasped her hands with agitation, wondering how best to broach the subject. Finally, she decided just to be blunt.

"Last Monday, when I was here cleaning house for Aunt Lois, I saw something."

"*Ja?*"

"It was here in your office." Emma gestured. "I dusted and swept. But I—I saw a file on your desk. A file on Thomas."

A strange expression crossed the older man's face, a blend of concern and amusement. "And let me guess. You saw his testimonial."

"Is that what it was? I read enough to scare me to death."

"Did you read the whole thing?"

"*N-nein.* I got nervous when you came home suddenly, so I stuffed everything back in and…and deliberately spilled ammonia in the kitchen."

Samuel's eyebrows shot into his hairline. "That was deliberate?"

"*Ja.* I was so…so shaken up by what I'd read that I needed a distraction to cover my tracks. F-forgive me, Uncle."

"But you didn't read the entire testimonial?"

"*Nein.* There wasn't enough time. But do I need to? Uncle Samuel, how can I allow myself to be courted by a man who committed involuntary manslaughter?"

"Is that what you think?" Samuel stood up, opened a file drawer, rummaged for a moment and withdrew a manila folder. He plopped it onto the desk and the contents half fanned out. The same letter she had seen before was visible on top.

He sat down and withdrew the multipage document and gave it to her. "Read it in full, Emma. Otherwise, you won't understand. I'll leave you for a few minutes while you do that." He rose from his seat and left the room.

In the sudden quiet, Emma stared at the neatly typewritten document for a moment and then yanked it toward her.

The first portion was as she remembered—a gut-clenching collection of transgressions, both large and small. And at the very end of the second page, that same line—"and then I was accused of involuntary manslaughter"—leaped out at her. Taking a deep breath, she turned the page over and continued reading. And reading. And reading.

Dear *Gott*, she had misjudged him. Far from doing something that had caused an innocent person to die, he had been nowhere near the scene.

That was an enormous relief, yes. But his heartfelt promise to both *Gott* and his brother, Joseph, to commit to a new course of life and someday pay forward the gift of grace he had been given when his name was cleared brought her to tears.

Without the cloud of dread over her, she realized with an agonizing twist of her heart that she was in serious danger of falling in love with Thomas. But she was still frightened, almost paralyzed with fear at making another mistake...

"Do you understand now?" said her uncle from the doorway.

She jumped. Caught unawares, she didn't have time to compose her expression before her uncle saw her. He sucked in his breath and caught one of her hands. "*Ach*, child, it's not as bad as that."

"Oh, Uncle, I'm so confused," she sobbed.

He squatted down next to her chair, and she leaned into his shoulder and gave way to tears. He patted her back and let her soak his shirt for a few minutes before she managed to compose herself and draw back, burying her face in the handkerchief she fished out of her apron pocket.

Uncle Samuel retreated to the chair behind his desk once again and gave her a moment to pull herself together. "Am I to understand you've had a bad week?" he understated with a glimmer of humor.

"*Ja*." She sniffed and blew her nose.

"Tell me what's troubling you. What were you thinking all week?"

Something inside Emma knew now was the time to confess her deepest, darkest fears. "It may not be directly related to Thomas," she admitted. "I'm scared, Uncle Samuel. You know what my first marriage was like, and how relieved I was to be released from it. But it shows I have poor judgment. What if I make the same mistake again? It's not that my feelings toward Thomas have changed after finding this letter. I'm still grateful to him. But can I marry him? Can I give Hannah a father like that?"

"Like what?"

Her uncle's simple question drew her up short. "What do you mean 'like what'?"

"Just what I said. If you were to marry Thomas, do you think he would be a *gut* father to her? Or do you think he would be abusive toward her? Neglectful? Hurtful?"

She knew he would never hurt her daughter, but she felt compelled to argue. "But what if she gets inspired by his bad deeds as she gets older? What if she turns into a rebellious *youngie*?"

"Like you?"

Emma's mouth dropped open and she stared at her uncle.

Into the silence, he continued in a stern voice. "You aren't blameless in this situation, Emma. Thomas has done some irresponsible things in his life, but he's turned himself around. Your first husband did some irresponsible things too. But, my dear niece, *so have you.* You've done some bad things, starting with getting pregnant out of wedlock and ending with reading some correspondence that was none of your business." His voice gentled. "But out of those bad things, *gut* things can come. Out of the deed of getting pregnant out of wedlock, you now have a wonderful daughter. Out of the deed of reading some correspondence that was none of your business, you now have a better understanding of a man who desperately wants to become a fully baptized member of the church."

"But…but…" Emma sputtered and then collected herself. "But even getting pregnant with Hannah was nothing next to everything else Thomas has done, even if he is innocent of involuntary manslaughter." She thumped her finger on the letter.

The older man shook his head. "Sin is sin in the eyes of *Gott*. You can't take something out of context and then blame someone for your conclusions," he warned. "Remember, by his fruits you shall know him. Would you deny him the opportunity to redeem himself in the eyes of *Gott* and man? Thomas came here for a fresh start. Has he ever given you any indication he hasn't followed through and left his past behind?"

"Well, no, but—"

"But nothing. It's not so much the sin, Emma, but what you do about it after the fact."

Her lip trembled. "Then you th-think we should get married?"

"I would never presume to suggest anything of the sort. As you well know, marriage is a lifelong commitment. The choice must be entirely up to you—and Thomas, if he's the one. You chose badly with your first marriage, though you did your best under the circumstances. But don't let fears from your first marriage stop you from recognizing a *gut* candidate for your second."

With a flash of insight, Emma realized she was guilty of the sin of pride. *Hochmut.* She had been proud of her independence after being widowed. Proud of her accomplishments that had allowed her to make a living for her and her little daughter. Proud of her solid placement in the church community. She had been so sure she simply didn't need a man.

Now she understood better. She may not *need* a man… but perhaps she *wanted* one.

Was her pride making it more difficult for Thomas to redeem himself? His humble accomplishments since arriving in Montana gave credence to what her uncle said. He wanted to create a new man in himself.

"It might make him a stronger man," she mused, and was startled when she said the words out loud.

"You mean because of the way he was in the past? *Ja*, it might." Her uncle smiled paternally at her. "Since you're on his journey of discovery, ask him why he was determined to help the *Englisch youngie* Jeremy Watson. It's a nice story."

"And you, Uncle, you were willing to take a chance on Thomas as well. Why?" Emma touched the letter on the desk. "Was it solely based on the strength of this testimonial?"

"Not solely, no. I also had a great deal of correspondence with his brother, Joseph, and his sister, Miriam, as well as the bishop of his old town in Indiana. All of them confirmed what Thomas was saying about his desire for a new life. I haven't been disappointed, Emma, and you shouldn't be, either. Thomas isn't the first to move to Montana to leave a painful past behind and find a new life. You might argue you've done the same thing, *ja*?"

"Ja." The tension that had been clenched inside Emma for the last week was gone, replaced with a sense of urgency to right the wrongs she had sowed. She rose. "Uncle, may I borrow your buggy? It seems I have some apologies to make."

"Ja, sure." The older man's eyes crinkled with amusement. "And maybe your aunt might like Hannah to stay here with us for an hour or two."

Emma walked over and kissed her uncle on the forehead. *"Danke*, Uncle Samuel." She hoped he understood just what kind of a gift he had offered her.

He nodded and rose. "*Komm.* I'll hitch up the horse for you. And you might explain to Hannah how much fun she'll have here with us."

Emma managed a chuckle. "She's much like me. Put her in the garden, and she'll be happy as a clam."

Thomas rattled around his room at the boardinghouse, depressed. His thoughts had taken another flip and, once again, he was giving serious thought to returning to Indiana. Or perhaps there was another far-flung church that might be willing to take a chance on him.

All the potential here in his new home was pointless without Emma. All his hard work, all the carefully cultivated professional relationships, all the strides and advances he had made, all the potential he had for his future—it counted for nothing if the woman he was interested in could fling his past in his face with such loathing.

But the thought of starting over again somewhere else was equally depressing. In the months leading up to the bishop accepting his petition to migrate to Montana, as well as the time he'd been here so far, he had put an enormous amount of emotional energy into the thought of rebuilding his life anew.

Now, he questioned whether it could ever be done. Would his past always haunt him? Would there be no woman able or willing to overlook it and give him a chance?

Should he have been forthright with Emma from the start? He clearly remembered the day in the park just before the car accident where Emma had revealed details about the situation with her first husband. He knew it had been cathartic for her to explain her fears and insecurities. But when she had wanted to know about his

past, as well, he'd refused to tell her. His own fears and
insecurities had been still too raw and fresh.

In retrospect, it had been a stunningly bad decision to
keep things secret from her. If he wanted a future with
Emma, it had to be based on truth and a thorough understanding of each other. Had he honestly thought he
could get away with never telling her anything about his
life before they'd met?

But his fears that she would turn away if she knew
the truth had proven correct. And now he wondered if
he wanted to remain in a church community where the
woman he loved—and the child he had come to adore—
would never look at him in the same way again.

There was a knock on his door. Matthew, no doubt.
Thomas debated ignoring it, but his landlord didn't deserve to be on the receiving end of Thomas's mental anguish. He sighed, strode over to the door and yanked it
open.

It was Emma.

Emma, with reddened eyes and an unfathomable expression on her face. Thomas was so startled to see her
that he froze, cautious and watchful. Several heartbeats
passed in silence.

"I've come to apologize," she stated without preamble.

He blinked in surprise and the knot of fear and anger
and remorse and worry inside him began to loosen.

Into the yawning quiet, she added, "There's a nice
walking path along a creek at the edge of town. It would
allow us a chance to talk." At his continued silence, a look
of fear crept into her eyes. "Say something, Thomas. Or
did I ruin any chance of a future with you?"

Something inside him snapped. He snatched her
into his arms and buried his face in her *kapp*. Her arms
wrapped around him as he clung to her, rocking slightly.

"I've been so worried," he whispered into her hair. "So desperately worried I'd lost you. I've been mulling over wild plans to leave town and go somewhere else. I didn't see how I could stay here if it meant I had to pretend I had no interest in you."

"Don't go," she breathed. "Please, Thomas, don't go. This week has been awful. Thinking I had mistaken the man I had fallen in love with…"

Half an hour later, Thomas strode hand in hand with Emma along a paved walking path next to a burbling creek. The path was deserted except for them.

"And that's how I saw the letter," she concluded her tale. "I was nearly caught when Uncle Samuel came home unexpectedly, so I didn't read the whole thing. Let me tell you, my uncle spent the last hour knocking some sense into my head…"

"*Gott* bless Uncle Samuel," murmured Thomas under his breath. He made a mental note to personally thank the bishop next time he saw him.

"And now I think I understand why you did what you did with Jeremy Watson," she continued. "It was to pay forward the gift your brother gave you, wasn't it?"

"*Ja*, exactly. If I could do anything to keep him from heading into the lifestyle I once had, it was worth it."

"Thomas…" Emma swung his hand clasped with hers. "I won't deny your past had me worried. I know it's not fair to judge you by things you've left behind, but still…"

Thomas felt a moment of sadness. "I can't change what's in my past any more than you can change what's in yours," he reminded her. "I'll always bear a scar on my face to remind me of what a bad man I was. I'm guessing you're worried I'll turn into your first *hutband*. But I'm *not* your first *hutband*. What I hope," he added, "is to be your second."

Her hand tightened around his. "What you may not know," she said softly, "is how my mind entirely changed about you after you saved Hannah's life. Until I got side-tracked by my fears after reading that letter, I had decided a man who would risk his life to save my daughter is a man whose courtship I would welcome."

"Really?" Thomas stopped and turned to her.

"*Ja*, really."

A cheeky magpie was the only witness to the kiss that followed.

Thomas laid his forehead against hers and gulped in some fresh air. "It's going to have to be a long court-ship," he warned. "I'm not baptized yet, and I have to go through all the classes first. Besides, I have nothing to offer you. No home, no horse or buggy, nothing. I have some work ahead of me before I can provide for a family."

She chuckled and locked her hands behind his neck, her brown eyes dancing. "Why do you think Uncle Samuel and Aunt Lois are so generously offering the use of that shed between our properties as an office? I think they were hopeful."

"*Ja*, that's the impression I got too."

"Besides, when the time comes, we have the cabin I'm living in."

"It won't be big enough when *bopplin* start arriving," he said with a smile.

"But it can be expanded."

"Oh, Emma…" Thomas dropped a feather-soft kiss on her lips. "I have not been a *gut* man. I've made so many mistakes. My whole life, I've been an outcast. I've spent years facing judgment and rejection from the people I love because of my own actions. It's still a lingering fear. But I can promise you this—it's all behind me. It's the future I'm looking forward to, and it's never been brighter."

"That makes two of us. I was so sure I could do it all on my own—to raise Hannah without a husband, to be known as a strong and competent woman. What I never realized is that strength and competence isn't proven by being single. It's funny," she added. "It's almost like Hannah chose you from the start. I've sometimes felt very young children are closer to *Gott* and understand things adults can't. I wonder if she saw you as her new father from the beginning, long before I did?"

"If she did, it's a responsibility I'm happy to accept. And someday, we'll have more *kinner* too."

"More *kinner*." Emma had a dreamy look in her eyes. "I've always wanted more but thought that was just a dream. I certainly didn't want more with my first *hutband*, but *kinner* with you would be wonderful, Thomas."

"I think we're in for a wonderful future, aren't we?" Thomas wrapped his arms around Emma and simply reveled in her closeness. He closed his eyes. *"Gott ist gut."*

* * * * *

Dear Reader,

Here's a motto for a simpler life: *Make good choices*. When you think about it, so many complications we face come from a failure to live up to those three small words. But no matter how many mistakes we've made in the past, it's possible to look forward to a better future—if only we make good choices next time.

This is a story of how two people made poor choices in their past, and how they were able to overcome those choices and look toward a brighter future. I love stories of redemption and forgiveness because we could all use some in our own lives, don't you think?

I love hearing from readers and welcome messages at patricelewis@protonmail.com.

Blessings,
Patrice

COMING NEXT MONTH FROM
Love Inspired

THE AMISH MARRIAGE ARRANGEMENT
Amish Country Matches • by Patricia Johns
Sarai Peachy is convinced that her *grossmammi* and their next-door neighbor are the perfect match. But the older man's grandson isn't so sure. When a storm forces the two to work together on repairs, will spending time with Arden Stoltzfus prove to Sarai that the former heartbreaker is a changed man?

THE AMISH NANNY'S PROMISE
by Amy Grochowski
Since the loss of his wife, Nick Weaver has relied on nanny Fern Beiler to care for him and his *kinner*. But when the community pushes them into a marriage of convenience, the simple arrangement grows more complicated. Will these two friends find love for a lifetime?

HER ALASKAN COMPANION
K-9 Companions • by Heidi McCahan
Moving to Alaska is the fresh start that pregnant widow Lexi Thomas has been looking for. But taking care of a rambunctious dog wasn't part of the plan. When an unlikely friendship blooms between her and the dog's owner, Heath Donovan, can she take a chance and risk her heart again?

THE RELUCTANT RANCHER
Lone Star Heritage • by Jolene Navarro
World-weary FBI agent Enzo Flores returns home to help his pregnant sister. When she goes into premature labor, he needs help to care for his nephew and the ranch. Will childhood rival Resa Espinoza step in to help and forgive their troubled past?

FALLING FOR THE FAMILY NEXT DOOR
Sage Creek • by Jennifer Slattery
Needing a fresh start, Daria Ellis moves to Texas with her niece and nephew. But it's more challenging than she ever imagined, especially with handsome cowboy Tyler Reyes living next door. When they clash over property lines, will it ruin everything or prove to be a blessing in disguise?

A HAVEN FOR HIS TWINS
by April Arrington
Deciding to right the wrongs of the past, former bull rider Holt Williams returns home to reclaim his twin sons. But Jessie Alden, the woman who's raised them all these years, isn't keen on the idea. Can he be trusted, or will he hurt his sons—and her—all over again?

LICNM0623

Get 3 FREE REWARDS!

We'll send you 2 FREE Books plus a FREE Mystery Gift.

FREE
Value Over
$20

Both the **Love Inspired®** and **Love Inspired® Suspense** series feature compelling novels filled with inspirational romance, faith, forgiveness and hope.

YES! Please send me 2 FREE novels from the Love Inspired or Love Inspired Suspense series and my FREE gift (gift is worth about $10 retail). After receiving them, if I don't wish to receive any more books, I can return the shipping statement marked "cancel." If I don't cancel, I will receive 6 brand-new Love Inspired Larger-Print books or Love Inspired Suspense Larger-Print books every month and be billed just $6.49 each in the U.S. or $6.74 each in Canada. That is a savings of at least 16% off the cover price. It's quite a bargain! Shipping and handling is just 50¢ per book in the U.S. and $1.25 per book in Canada.* I understand that accepting the 2 free books and gift places me under no obligation to buy anything. I can always return a shipment and cancel at any time by calling the number below. The free books and gift are mine to keep no matter what I decide.

Choose one: ☐ **Love Inspired Larger-Print** (122/322 BPA GRPA)   ☐ **Love Inspired Suspense Larger-Print** (107/307 BPA GRPA)   ☐ **Or Try Both!** (122/322 & 107/307 BPA GRRP)

Name (please print)

Address   Apt. #

City   State/Province   Zip/Postal Code

Email: Please check this box ☐ if you would like to receive newsletters and promotional emails from Harlequin Enterprises ULC and its affiliates. You can unsubscribe anytime.

> Mail to the **Harlequin Reader Service:**
> **IN U.S.A.:** P.O. Box 1341, Buffalo, NY 14240-8531
> **IN CANADA:** P.O. Box 603, Fort Erie, Ontario L2A 5X3

Want to try 2 free books from another series! Call 1-800-873-8635 or visit www.ReaderService.com.

*Terms and prices subject to change without notice. Prices do not include sales taxes, which will be charged (if applicable) based on your state or country of residence. Canadian residents will be charged applicable taxes. Offer not valid in Quebec. This offer is limited to one order per household. Books received may not be as shown. Not valid for current subscribers to the Love Inspired or Love Inspired Suspense series. All orders subject to approval. Credit or debit balances in a customer's account(s) may be offset by any other outstanding balance owed by or to the customer. Please allow 4 to 6 weeks for delivery. Offer available while quantities last.

Your Privacy—Your information is being collected by Harlequin Enterprises ULC, operating as Harlequin Reader Service. For a complete summary of the information we collect, how we use this information and to whom it is disclosed, please visit our privacy notice located at corporate.harlequin.com/privacy-notice. From time to time we may also exchange your personal information with reputable third parties. If you wish to opt out of this sharing of your personal information, please visit readerservice.com/consumerchoice or call 1-800-873-8635. **Notice to California Residents**—Under California law, you have specific rights to control and access your data. For more information on these rights and how to exercise them, visit corporate.harlequin.com/california-privacy.

LIRLIS23

HARLEQUIN
PLUS

Try the best multimedia subscription service for romance readers like you!

Read, Watch and Play.

Experience the easiest way to get the romance content you crave.

Start your **FREE TRIAL** at
www.harlequinplus.com/freetrial.